I SCREAM

A SEASIDE ICE CREAM SHOP MYSTERY (BOOK 2)

ANGELA K. RYAN

JOHN PAUL PUBLISHING

Copyright © 2022 by Angela K. Ryan

All rights reserved.

No part of this book may be reproduced in any form or by any electronic or mechanical means, including information storage and retrieval systems, without written permission from the author, except for the use of brief quotations in a book review.

Publisher's Note: This is a work of fiction. Names, characters, places, and incidents are a product of the author's imagination. Locales and public names are sometimes used for atmospheric purposes. Any resemblance to actual people, living or deceased, or to businesses, companies, events, institutions or locales is completely coincidental.

Cover Design © 2021 MariahSinclair.com

I Scream/Angela K. Ryan. -- 1st ed.

ISBN: 978-1-7367867-8-9

CHAPTER 1

*A*nna clutched her cell phone as she walked briskly toward the cove, eager to receive her cousin Connie's phone call. The two had arranged to talk at 8:00 on Monday morning, so they could discuss a topic which could prove to be of monumental importance - the possibility that Anna's sister Bella might still be alive.

When Anna arrived at the cove, she kicked off her flip flops and carried them across the coarse brown sand toward a jetty on the other side. Stepping onto the New England beach was like walking through a portal into a different world. The carefree sounds of children laughing and seagulls calling out to one another filled Anna's ears as the sun in the clear July sky warmed her skin. A few feet away, crashing waves sent small children squealing as they ran away from the ocean with flailing arms.

A colony of seagulls flew away as Anna walked in their direction. She watched as they landed on a section of one of the jetties where they wouldn't be disturbed by excited children.

As Anna climbed onto the jetty, she smiled at the sight of a young boy watching with excitement as a man with bronzed skin and sun-bleached hair cast a fishing rod from a rock twenty feet away from the shore.

Anna found a smooth rock far enough from the shore, so that she wouldn't have to worry about anyone overhearing her conversation with her cousin. Not that anyone would be interested enough to eavesdrop, but still, it was hard enough for Anna to talk about this subject with her cousin, never mind knowing strangers might overhear her.

There were two beaches in Seagull Cove, Massachusetts. The first, which was a short walk from the downtown area, was a cove, and the other was a long stretch of beach appropriately called "Mile Long Beach."

Just as Anna settled onto one of the rocks, her phone rang, and Connie's name popped onto her screen.

"Connie!" Anna answered before the first ring ended.

"It's great to hear your voice, Anna! I hear you've been keeping yourself busy in Seagull Cove. Gianna has been keeping me posted."

"You mean about the murder that happened right after my grand opening," Anna said.

"I mean exactly that. I guess this sleuthing gene runs in the family. Who would have imagined that?"

Anna chuckled. "I definitely didn't go looking for it. The murder case came to me."

"That's how it all starts," Connie warned.

"How is married life treating you, little cousin?"

Anna could practically hear the smile on the other end of the line. "It's even more amazing than I thought it would be.

Of course, there are some adjustments, especially since I waited until I was thirty-seven to get married, but Zach is great."

Anna's heart swelled. "I'm so happy for you, Connie."

"So, I'm dying of curiosity. What could possibly be so urgent that you wanted to talk as soon as possible? Don't tell me you're involved in another investigation, and you're stuck," Connie said.

"Well… not exactly. It's more like an old investigation that you know about all too well."

There was a loud silence on the other end of the line as Anna gave Connie a moment to process what she had just said.

"You're talking about Bella," Connie said. "I had a feeling that once you settled into Seagull Cove, you'd start poking around the details surrounding her death. When we talked last November, it was clear that you had some suspicions regarding Bella's death." When Anna had been in Florida for Connie's wedding, they discussed Anna's unresolved questions about her sister's boating accident.

"Promise me that you won't breathe a word of what I'm doing to anyone," Anna said. "I don't want the whole family worrying about me and thinking I'm delusional. I wouldn't put it past my parents to leave their retirement home in New Hampshire and move to Seagull Cove just to keep an eye on me."

"I promise, Anna. It will be our secret."

"I considered confiding in Gianna, but she's so busy with the twins, and I don't want to worry her. She'd feel compelled to help me, and this is something I need to do alone."

"I understand. You're probably right. But if you should ever need a shoulder to lean on, she's a strong woman."

"I know. We'll see what happens. I'll eventually catch her up on things, especially if I have more to report. For now, I don't want her to be worried. Or worse, to get her hopes up."

"Like yours are?" Connie asked.

"I have to admit, I've discovered a few things that have raised my hopes that Bella could be alive. I thought you would be the perfect person to bounce them off."

"Before we get into the details, I hear that your shop is a smashing success," Connie said. "Congratulations!"

"It was slow going the first couple of weeks because of Marcus's murder. But ever since Old Joe Wiggins and I solved the case, the store has been super busy."

"Old Joe Wiggins?"

Anna chuckled. "Yeah. He's only sixty, but he has an old soul, so that's what a lot of people in town call him. He's actually quite youthful in some ways."

"I love it."

"Joe is a retired private investigator, so that's been helpful, both with Marcus's murder and with the mystery of Bella's accident. He lives above my shop."

"That's great!" Connie said. "It sounds like you've already made some great friends in Seagull Cove." Anna briefly told her about Velma, Sonja, Rosie, Ruthie, and the others whom she had enjoyed getting to know.

"So, before I collapse of suspense, tell me what makes you think Bella could still be alive."

Anna took a deep breath and shifted on the hard rock.

"At the grand opening of my ice cream shop on Memorial

Day Weekend, I met Joe Wiggins. He asked why my shop was named *Bella's Dream* if my name was Anna."

"That's a logical question," Connie said.

"For sure. I told him about Bella's boating accident and how it had always been her dream to open an ice cream shop that hosted opportunities for the community to gather. Then I brought him to a framed picture of Bella, which hangs by the counter. He informed me that he thought he saw Bella across the street on the morning of my grand opening."

"What?! He *had* to have been mistaken."

"That was my initial thought, but Velma assured me that Joe has a sharp eye. They've been friends since they were kids, and she said that he has always had keen observation skills, which were further sharpened during his career as a P.I. He's a trustworthy source. Of course, he said he couldn't be sure it was Bella and encouraged me to forget what he said, once he found out about Bella's boating accident. But how can I, Connie, if there's even a glimmer of hope?"

"That doesn't make sense, though. Why would Bella come within feet of your shop and not reveal herself? If she *is* alive, that would not only mean that she is following your life, but that she is free to go wherever she wants."

"I have no idea, Connie. It would likely mean that she staged her death and wants everyone to believe she is dead, but I can't imagine why she would do that. It's not like she has some sort of shady past. If she had been a lawyer who prosecuted members of the Mafia, or something like that, it would make more sense. It truly is puzzling. I managed to convince Joe to come with me by boat to the spot of her accident."

"What did he say about it?"

"He said that if someone were going to stage their own

death, that would be the perfect place to do it. Bella's body wasn't found, and the location of her accident wasn't that far from shore. She easily could have staged the accident and swam to shore. And that's not all. I outright asked Joe whether if Bella were his sister, he would investigate further."

"And?"

"He said that he'd feel compelled to find answers."

There was a long silence.

"Connie, are you there?"

"Yeah, I'm here. Wow."

"It's still a long shot, Connie, but I have to pursue this."

"I can't say that I blame you. If it were Gi, I would feel the same way."

"I knew you'd understand. But promise me again that you won't tell any of our parents."

"I promise," Connie said. "But *you* have to promise *me* that you'll be careful. You could be walking into an extremely dangerous situation." Connie let out a sharp breath. "It's ironic, I'm usually on the receiving end of that advice. Now I understand why everyone is always worried about me whenever I'm working on a case."

"I promise. Even though I've only known Joe for a short time, he watches out for me."

"That takes a load off my mind," Connie said.

"I feel better already, Connie. I needed to say all this aloud to someone who knows me well and who also knew Bella. And someone with some mad sleuthing skills," Anna added. "What do you think I should do next? I've been contemplating my next move for more than a month, and I'm stuck."

Connie let out another deep breath. "I don't know, Anna. Can you talk to the police about your suspicions?"

"Not yet. I think I need some evidence before I do that. Or at least more information."

"You're probably right," Connie said. "Hey, I just had a thought. Wasn't there a reporter who covered Bella's boating accident? I can't think of his name, but I remember reading his articles. Your parents once said that they personally thanked him for his compassionate coverage of the investigation and for respecting their privacy during the initial days after the accident."

"You're right," Anna said. "I can't remember his name, either, but I'm sure I can find it easily enough. His articles should be archived at the library."

"I would start there," Connie said.

Anna took a deep breath. "This is going to be hard. I haven't read those articles since the accident more than four years ago."

"Are you sure you're up for it?" Connie asked.

"It'll be tough, but it's something I need to do. Maybe if I read them with new eyes, it will spark something. At the very least, I can find the name of the reporter. Thanks, Connie. That's what I'm going to do."

"If you need anything, including just a shoulder to lean on, call any time."

"Thanks. And I hope to see you in Seagull Cove sometime in the near future. Perhaps you and Zach could take a second honeymoon."

"I'd love that," Connie said. "Right now, I'm sitting by the pier looking out at the Gulf of Mexico."

Anna smiled. "And I'm down at the cove looking onto the Atlantic Ocean."

"I'll grab my paddle board and meet you for lunch," Connie

said, jokingly.

"Great, I'll see you at noon!"

"Love you, Anna."

"Love you, too, Connie. And thanks."

By the time her conversation with her cousin ended, Anna felt as if a weight had been lifted from her shoulders. She now had a plan.

There were still more than two hours before Anna needed to open *Bella's Dream*. Judging from what promised to be another hot day, Anna fully expected to be busy from opening until closing. The hot summer weather was definitely good for the ice cream business.

There was no point in putting off her difficult task. She started walking toward the library to begin rereading the articles on Bella's death and to find the name of the reporter who covered it. She strolled up Main Street and had just passed her shop when she heard a loud, piercing scream.

Anna's walk turned into a jog as she rushed in the direction of the scream. But she couldn't tell where exactly it came from.

Anna frantically scanned the area. After a few seconds, she looked up at the window of an office located above a clothing boutique and discovered the source of the scream. It was Olivia, one of her high-school-aged employees. The young woman sobbed as she covered her face with her hands.

Anna pushed open the green wooden door that led to a staircase, which she hoped would bring her to where Olivia was standing. She took the stairs two by two and burst through the door to the second floor office. It didn't take long to see what caused Olivia's reaction.

On the floor in front of a large wooden desk was a man

who appeared to be in his late twenties, surrounded by blood. Anna went over to check his pulse, but it was pointless. The man was dead.

Anna looked up at Olivia. "I'm so sorry."

Tears streamed from the teenager's brown eyes. "That's my Uncle Luke."

CHAPTER 2

Anna rushed toward Olivia, and, placing her arm around the teenager's shoulders, turned her away from her uncle's corpse. Olivia's body trembled beneath Anna's arm.

"What are you doing here?" Anna asked.

"This is my uncle's office. My mother sent me to pick something up that she left at his house last night. When I got here, I found him like this."

The first thing Anna did was call 9-1-1. Then she glanced around the office.

The furniture in the office was sparse. The wooden desk, which was placed in the center of the room, faced the door. Two wingbacked chairs were set up conversation style, facing the desk. In addition to the front door, which Anna had come through, there was a back door leading to a fire escape.

As she was comforting Olivia, Anna surveyed the rest of the small office. The body was on the floor between the desk and the back exit. Lying next to it was a golf club, which, as far as Anna could tell with her limited knowledge of golf, looked to be a driver. The business end was covered with blood. Fortunately for Olivia, the body was on its stomach, and not all of the wounds were fully visible, but it was clear that Luke had been struck multiple times with the club.

Anna noticed a white bowl with the name "Casper" printed on it in royal blue on the floor next to the back door. Casper was a feral cat that Anna, as well as many of the business owners on Main Street, had befriended. A lump formed in Anna's throat as she realized that, not only was the victim Olivia's uncle, but he had been a friend of Casper's.

Her observations were interrupted by a new wave of sobbing from Olivia, whose head was now buried in Anna's shoulder. She caressed the teen's head. As Anna was trying to decide whether to remove Olivia from the scene or to wait there until the police arrived, she heard a siren approaching in the distance.

Within a couple of minutes, two EMTs were racing onto the scene, followed right after by Joe Wiggins.

Anna motioned to Joe that she was going to take Olivia to *Bella's Dream*. The shop wasn't due to open for another couple of hours, so there would be plenty of privacy. Somehow Anna needed to calm the distraught teen.

"Can you tell Charlie where we'll be?" Anna asked. She knew Detective Charlie Doyle would arrive at any moment, but she needed to get Olivia out of there.

Joe nodded solemnly.

She ushered Olivia across the street and into *Bella's Dream*. "I'm so sorry about your uncle, Olivia," Anna said with her arm still draped around the teenager's shoulders. "Why don't we call your mother?"

Olivia nodded and handed Anna her cell phone. "I can't do

it. I don't think I'll be able to get the words out. Will you call her for me?"

"Of course I will."

Olivia called up the contact that said "Mom" and handed the phone to Anna. "She's down at Mile Long Beach taking a walk, so she's not that far away."

"At least she won't have to drive." Anna said a silent prayer for the strength to break this awful news to Olivia's mother and pressed the call button.

"Hi, honey," came a woman's voice through the phone.

"Mrs. Montgomery, this is Anna McBride, Olivia's employer."

"Oh, yes, hi, Anna. Please, call me Ellen." Then her tone changed. "Wait, why are you calling me on my daughter's phone? Is Olivia okay?"

"Yes, Olivia is completely fine. I mean, nothing has happened to *Olivia*. I mean, *physically* she is okay." This wasn't going well. Anna took a deep breath. "Olivia is safe and sound, but I'm afraid I have some bad news about Olivia's uncle, Luke," Anna said, since she was unsure if Luke was Ellen's brother or brother-in-law.

"What happened to Luke?" Ellen asked.

"I'm afraid that Luke was attacked," Anna preferred to tell Ellen in person that he had been killed, if possible. "Could you come to *Bella's Dream* right away? Olivia is quite upset."

"Is Luke okay? Should I meet him at the hospital?"

Anna swallowed hard. "That won't be necessary. Why don't you come to my shop, and we can talk in person?"

Ellen disconnected the call, and within five minutes a woman whom Anna presumed to be Ellen, was jogging down the street in the direction of *Bella's Dream*. She stopped in front of the shop, and Anna and Olivia went out to the sidewalk to meet her. Ellen's eyes darted between Olivia and the scene across the street, which now included two police cars, as well as a truck from Seagull Cove Fire Rescue. A police officer was taping off the scene around the building with yellow crime-scene tape.

Ellen sprinted in the direction of the crime scene.

Anna stepped outside and called her name, but it was too late. Ellen had already crossed the street, causing the driver of an oncoming car to sound its horn, as he narrowly missed Ellen.

Anna watched heavy-hearted as Ellen broke through the tape and raced into the building that housed Luke's office. The police officer chased after her. Anna hoped that either the police or Joe would stop her before she saw the body.

Olivia started toward the building, but Anna stopped her. "Don't go back in there, Olivia. Someone will bring your mother to you."

Sure enough, within a couple of minutes, Detective Charlie Doyle was escorting Ellen across the street and toward *Bella's Dream*. Charlie, too, looked as if he were on the verge of tears.

"I am so sorry, Ellen," Anna said, meeting Ellen halfway across the street. She looped her arm through the distraught woman's, so that she could help Charlie accompany her toward the shop.

Olivia ran to her mother as soon as they reached the sidewalk, and the two broke down in each other's arms.

Anna had to choke back the tears as she watched the mother and daughter grieve their loved one. She couldn't help but think of the times she had been on the receiving end of news like that. First after her fiancé Ian's fatal car accident. Then, six years later, when she received the news of Bella's boating accident.

All four went inside and sat at a table in the dining room. Anna brought Olivia and her mother each a glass of water and placed a box of tissues on the table.

Anna's ice cream shop had two sections. One contained the ice cream counter and cash register, with a small office in back. It had floor-to-ceiling windows, which overlooked Main Street, with a glass door in the middle. There was a small bistro table in front of each window. A cased opening separated the first section from a spacious dining room. It also had floor-to-ceiling windows facing Main Street. The far wall was lined with booths, while rectangular wooden tables were sprinkled throughout the rest of the room.

Ellen and Olivia were sitting at a four-top in the middle of the dining room. They sat next to one another, facing the windows and watching the flurry of activity that was taking place across the street. Anna and Charlie sat across from them.

"We need to call Dad," Olivia said.

"Let's give him a few minutes. He's dropping off your brother and sister at summer camp right now. We should wait until he's done."

Olivia nodded.

"Ellen, I need to get back across the street," Charlie said. "I'll come back here as soon as I can."

Anna glanced at the strawberry ice cream cone wall clock. It was only 9:30. At least they still had some time before she had to open the shop.

"I'm so sorry," Anna said, after Charlie left. "I know there are no words that can bring you comfort."

"Things were going so well for Uncle Luke," Olivia said.

"I know, sweetie." Ellen looked blankly at Anna. "My little brother got himself into some trouble a few years ago, but he had pulled himself out of it. We were all so proud of him, and optimistic about his future."

Olivia looked directly into Anna's eyes. "Someone murdered him, didn't they, Anna?"

"How would Anna know that?" Ellen asked. Then, a look of understanding spread across her face. "Oh, that's right. You and Old Joe solved Marcus Grady's murder. I suppose you know a thing or two about murder."

"I wouldn't say that. That was the first investigation I was ever involved with, and I had a lot of help from Joe. I'm sure Charlie will tell you more as soon as he can. Did you see the body?"

Ellen shook her head. "Charlie stopped me before I could get in there."

"I think it's safe to say that your brother was murdered," Anna said. *Nobody could do that to himself.*

"It had to be somebody from his past," Olivia said. "I'll bet Nina killed my uncle."

Anna gave them a puzzled look.

"As I said before, my brother got into some trouble a few years ago. To make a long story short, when Luke was in college, he injured his back pretty badly in a football game. He eventually underwent surgery, and his back mended, but he ended up with an addiction to the painkillers he had been prescribed. That led to a couple of bad years, but last year, he finally sought the help that he needed."

"It was awful," Olivia said. "Those were terrible years. I was young, but I remember it all. Uncle Luke wasn't himself for a long time. We barely heard from him during that time."

"When he finally reached back out to us, he had hit bottom and checked himself into a detox facility," Ellen said. "He moved in with us for little while after he finished the program. He got his life back on track, made amends to all those he hurt, and, a year ago, he embarked on a career as an independent insurance agent. We were all hoping this would be a new beginning for him."

"Even Detective Doyle was proud of him," Olivia said.

"That's right," Ellen said. "Charlie took Luke under his wing once he got out of rehab. They've been having breakfast together once a week before work ever since. Charlie was a true mentor for Luke."

That explained why Charlie had looked as if he were having a hard time keeping it together.

"Who is Nina?" Anna asked.

"She's Luke's ex-girlfriend," Ellen said. "They were together during the time that Luke was addicted to drugs. She recently tried to get back together with him, but Luke had already moved on."

"Has Nina cleaned up her life?" Anna asked.

Ellen nodded. "According to Luke, she checked herself into a rehab shortly after he did. But I'm glad they didn't get back together. She was never right for my brother, even if she had gotten clean. According to Luke, she didn't take it well that he refused to get back together. But why would he? He was happy with his new girlfriend." A fresh wave of tears streamed down Ellen's face. "Nicole is going to be devastated."

Anna was about to ask whether Ellen and Olivia knew of

any other enemies that Luke had, but she bit her tongue. There was no reason to ask. Anna was *not* getting involved in another murder investigation. Marcus Grady's case was a one-time thing, because it directly affected her ice cream shop. Besides, she had too much on her plate with her new business and her questions about Bella's accident.

Not to mention that Joe would never go for it. She wouldn't investigate alone, and she would already be pushing her luck when she asked if Joe would come with her to talk to the journalist who covered Bella's death.

She didn't dare ask him for two major favors.

CHAPTER 3

At about 10:30, Charlie trudged back to *Bella's Dream*. Although he had only arrived on the scene a couple of hours ago, he looked as though he had been working all night.

"You look like you could use a break," Anna said, pulling out a chair across from Ellen and Olivia. "Sit down, and I'll get you some water."

Charlie nodded and sat while Anna fetched four bottles of water from the mini-fridge in her office.

When she returned, Ellen was asking Charlie who he thought did this to Luke.

Charlie shook his head. "I wish I could tell you. I just don't understand. Everything seemed to be going so well for Luke. His business was beginning to take off, and he had a girlfriend whom he loved and who was good for him."

"I like her, too," Olivia said.

"Charlie was a godsend during those first few fragile months, after Luke came home," Ellen said. "Just knowing that

Luke had someone outside the family looking out for him was such a relief."

Charlie swallowed hard. "It was a privilege. I enjoyed our weekly breakfasts. Luke was trying hard to make up for the past few years. Nothing was more important to him than being a good boyfriend to Nicole and a good brother and uncle to you two. He was becoming a real asset to the Seagull Cove community."

Olivia rested her head on her mother's shoulder.

"I'm so sorry," was all that Anna could think of to say. Moments like these were particularly challenging, because they brought to the surface Anna's own grief.

While they were talking, Velma arrived for her shift.

Ellen pulled her cell phone from her pocket and glanced at the time. "I didn't realize it was so late. You're opening in five minutes. Why don't we leave you to it?"

Velma gave Olivia a comforting hug. "I'm so sorry, Olivia. I heard what happened."

Olivia returned her hug.

"We'd better drive to your father's office and break the news to him," Ellen said. "I don't want him hearing about this from anyone else."

"Mom, I'm scheduled to work at 11:00," Olivia said.

"I'm sure Anna doesn't expect you to work today, sweetie."

"Of course not. Don't even think about it, Olivia. Take as much time off as you need."

"We'll get coverage for your shifts," Velma said. "Right now, you need to be with your family."

"Well, okay then. You're probably right. My brother and sister are going to be crushed when they hear that Uncle Luke died. I should be there for them."

Alex, Anna's other employee who was scheduled that day, came in next.

"I guess we should go, then," Ellen said, and the two somberly walked out the door.

"I should get back over there, too," Charlie said. "It's going to be a long day."

Alex looked at Anna and Velma with a confused expression. "What happened across the street? One of the buildings is taped off like some sort of crime scene."

Anna recounted to Alex what happened.

"You mean Olivia found her own uncle's body?"

Anna nodded.

"The poor kid," Velma said. "I hadn't heard that part. I only heard that her uncle, Luke had been found dead, and, judging from the crime scene tape, I gathered that the circumstances were suspicious. I didn't know Luke well, but Seagull Cove is a small town, so I knew him in passing. He used to come into the ice cream shop years ago, when it belonged to the previous owners. I know he had his struggles in the past, but he seemed to be building a good life for himself."

Alex stood up and walked over to the window. "It's getting hot out there, so we are probably in for a busy day. I'll text Trish and see if she can work."

"Thanks, Alex," Anna said. "That would be great."

Within a half hour, Trish had arrived, and she, Alex, and Velma were working like a well-oiled machine behind the counter. Velma was at her usual post at the register, while college students Alex and Trish filled the orders. When the line got particularly long, Anna also hopped behind the counter to speed things along, but for the most part, her employees had things under control.

There was a heaviness in the air, which lingered even as the afternoon wore on. By the time Joe Wiggins came in for his daily scoop of chocolate chip ice cream at 2:30, it felt as if it should be closing time already.

"It looks like the police are still hard at work across the street," Anna said when she placed a bowl of ice cream in front of him, along with a cup of water.

"I was talking with Charlie before I came in here. They'll be at it for a while." He shook his head. "This is going to be a tough one for Charlie."

As usual, Joe enjoyed some good-spirited banter with Anna's college-aged employees in between customers.

"Only tourists and old folks are as tan as you are, Joe," Alex said.

Joe pretended to be insulted and turned his back toward Alex.

When Joe was about to leave, Anna approached him, pulling off her blue apron. "Could I talk to you for a quick second, Joe?"

"Please don't tell me that you want to talk about Luke's murder investigation," he groaned. "You don't have a direct connection to this one, so you have no reason to get involved. Remember the dangerous situation we put ourselves in the last time we investigated?"

"Don't worry, Joe. Nothing could be further from my mind."

"Glad to hear it."

"Could I walk with you for a minute?"

"Sure, knock yourself out. I have to stop at the pharmacy up the street," he said, turning right onto Main Street.

"It's about Bella."

Joe slowed his pace. "I was wondering where you were with all that. You haven't brought it up since our little boating excursion last month."

"I know. I've been giving some thought to what my next move should be. I think I'm going to go to the library tomorrow morning and reread the newspaper articles surrounding Bella's death. I also wanted to get the name of the journalist who covered the investigation."

"That sounds like the next logical step," Joe said. "I know most of the journalists in this town. Let me know who it turns out to be. I can at least tell you who you'll be dealing with before you call him or her."

"Thanks, Joe, I appreciate that. In fact, I was on my way to the library this morning when I found Olivia, so of course I spent the rest of the morning with her and her mother."

"Just be careful, kiddo. You could be opening a can of worms. If your sister should happen to be alive, there's a reason she's in hiding."

"I know. I'll be careful." Even as Anna said the words, she wasn't sure exactly how she would go about doing that. As far as Anna could tell, she had two choices. Investigate, or don't investigate. And if there was even the slightest chance that Joe really had seen Anna on the morning of her grand opening, the choice was a no-brainer.

Joe continued up Main Street, and Anna walked back to *Bella's Dream.*

A long line had developed, so Anna got to work behind the counter. It was great to see business going strong after her rocky start back in May. Velma had turned out to be a fantastic manager. The younger and less-experienced employees responded well to having someone in charge when Anna wasn't there, and Anna loved that she could leave the shop for longer periods of time, and even take days off here and there.

The shift changed at 5:00, and three new employees arrived for the evening, which went by more quickly than the day shift. By 10:00, Anna's employees had cleaned the shop and were leaving for the night.

"Aren't you coming?" a high school student named Jack asked on his way out the door.

"It was such a busy night that I forgot to feed Casper." Anna walked her employees to the door so she could flip the "open" sign to "closed."

Jack chuckled as he left. "That cat has it made."

Anna didn't mention to Jack that she had spotted a cat food bowl with Casper's name on it in Luke's office, so tonight of all nights, she needed to take care of her feral friend.

Anna glanced across the street as she closed the door behind Jack. The police were still hard at work.

She scooped a can of chicken into Casper's bowl and brought it to the back door. The orange cat was sitting on the stoop waiting for her to emerge. Anna scratched the top of his head, put the bowl on the ground, and sat on the stoop while Casper ate his dinner. She waited for him to eat, rather than leaving the bowl out back until the morning, but Casper stopped eating after a few bites.

She wondered if he sensed that something was amiss on Main Street.

"Hello, Anna, are you here?" came a woman's voice from inside her shop. It sounded vaguely familiar, but Anna couldn't immediately place it. She got up and went inside the shop. It was Ellen.

"I saw your lights on. I was hoping you might still be here."

"Hi, Ellen. I was just waiting for Casper to finish his dinner."

Ellen stepped into the dining room and looked around. "I don't see anyone in here."

Anna chuckled. "Casper is a feral cat. He was eating in the alley out back, although he seems to have lost his appetite." Anna brought Ellen to the back door so she could see for herself.

Ellen smiled at the sight of the orange cat looking up at the women with his piercing green eyes.

"Casper has a way of showing up when people need him most," Anna said. "Many of the shop owners on Main Street feed him. He sort of belongs to everyone and no one, all at the same time, which works out well for me. I'd love to have a pet but am not home enough to take care of one. He seems to appear out of nowhere when you need him, and then he disappears again. That's why we call him Casper."

Ellen smiled halfheartedly. "Come to think of it, I think I remember Luke talking about him." Her expression suddenly grew serious again. "Speaking of Luke, I was hoping I could talk with you for a few minutes."

"Of course." Anna grabbed two folding chairs and brought them out back so they could sit outside. She hoped that with a little more time, Casper might finish his supper.

"I'm sorry to bother you so late." Dark circles had developed beneath Ellen's eyes.

"It's no problem at all. How is Olivia?"

"She's hanging in there. Olivia has been wonderful with

her younger brother and sister. They are seven and nine years old. We obviously didn't tell them all the details of what happened, since they are so young, but they know that Uncle Luke is in Heaven. Olivia played with them for most of the day, keeping them busy so that my husband, Caleb, and I could talk to friends and family, and to the police."

"I'm not surprised. Olivia is a mature and sensitive young woman."

"She reminded me again of how you and Old Joe Wiggins solved the murder of Marcus Grady. By the way, I'm sorry that I forced Olivia to quit her job in *Bella's Dream* after he was killed. Her father and I thought we were doing the right thing at the time, but in hindsight, Marcus's murder had nothing to do with you or your shop."

"Don't even mention it," Anna said. "I completely understand why you made that decision."

"I'm glad there are no hard feelings. The reason I came by tonight is somewhat connected to Marcus's murder."

Anna hoped that Ellen wasn't about to ask what she thought she was going to ask.

"Since you seem to have a knack for solving murders, I was wondering if you might consider helping me find Luke's killer."

CHAPTER 4

There it was. The one question that Anna hoped Ellen wouldn't ask.

"I don't know what to say, Ellen. The only reason I investigated Marcus's death was because of the direct impact it had on my business. I don't know anything about criminal justice. Besides, Charlie is perfectly capable. I know it's hard to be patient, but just give him some time."

"Oh, I know that Charlie is a good detective. I was just thinking that the more eyes on the case, the better," Ellen said. "And Olivia tells me that you owned a counseling practice in Boston before moving to Seagull Cove, so you're obviously a student of human behavior."

"Well, that's true. But there's a lot more to solving crimes than having a good understanding of human behavior. Joe Wiggins and I almost got ourselves killed in June. He made it abundantly clear that helping me with a murder investigation was a one-time thing. He only agreed to help me because my sister's dream was slipping through my hands."

"Olivia told me about Bella. I'm so sorry. I admire what you're doing with this ice cream shop in your sister's memory."

Anna forced a smile. "Thank you."

"Perhaps when the dust settles and I know what happened to my brother, I can think about doing something to honor Luke's memory, as you have done for your sister."

"I'm sure you'll think of something when the time is right. My sister died more than four years ago, and I just recently opened *Bella's Dream*. It can take time."

"See, you understand exactly what I'm going through. Even though your sister wasn't murdered, she was taken from you much too early. You are one of the few people I know who has any idea what this feels like. If Luke were *your* brother, wouldn't you be pulling out all the stops to find out what happened? If you thought your sister's death might not be an accident, wouldn't you look for answers?"

Ouch. That question hit close to home.

Anna didn't even have to think about the answer. Little did Ellen know that she was facing that exact scenario, and she had already made the decision to investigate.

Casper, who still hadn't finished his dinner, hopped onto Anna's lap. His big green eyes seemed to be condemning her for refusing to help Ellen.

Anna tried to ignore him. "I understand where you're coming from, Ellen. Really I do."

"Then don't give me an answer now. I'll stop by tomorrow afternoon, and we can talk again."

"I don't think…"

Ellen interrupted her. "If you decide not to help, I'll

completely understand. There won't be any hard feelings. Just promise me you won't give me an answer until you sleep on it."

"I guess I can agree to that," Anna said. Although she didn't imagine that one night's sleep would make any difference, she didn't have the heart to turn Ellen down right away. Not after the day Ellen had.

Plus, Casper was still looking at her with those pleading green eyes.

"That's all I ask. Thank you, Anna. I'd better be going. I told my family that I was going out to get some air, and I don't want them to worry about me."

Casper hopped off Anna's lap and disappeared into the darkness, leaving behind his half-eaten bowl of chicken. After the women brought the folding chairs back inside, Anna cleaned the cat bowl and closed the shop. The two women left together.

It was a warm, pleasant evening, perfect for the short walk home. Anna tried unsuccessfully to push Ellen's request out of her mind. She chuckled to herself as she thought of her cousin Connie's words to her earlier that morning about murder investigations. Connie said that she never went looking for cases, but they always found their way to her. Anna was beginning to understand what she meant.

Anna woke up early on Tuesday morning, determined to get to the library to do some research on Bella's accident. She watered her small English garden, then had her morning coffee on the front porch. She had finally purchased some outdoor furniture at a Fourth of July sale that one of the local small businesses had run. She bought two dark brown wicker chairs with yellow cushions, which contrasted nicely against her light blue house, and a round table to go in the middle. Sometimes she came home in the middle of the day to have lunch on her porch and to escape the downtown busyness that the summer season brought. It had quickly become her favorite summer spot.

After a leisurely breakfast and a second cup of coffee, Anna headed to the library. *Seagull Cove Public Library* was located a few streets back from Main Street but further north than Anna's house. Anna decided to walk instead of bothering with her car.

She entered the substantial red brick structure and a friendly librarian brought her to the section that contained the microfilm machines, where Anna could view back issues of the local weekly newspaper, the *Seagull Cove Chronicle*. The librarian handed her the film that contained the newspapers during the time period that Anna was looking for. After a quick tutorial, she left her to her research.

Anna took a deep breath before reading the first article about Bella's accident. Then she moved on to the next. She proceeded to read every related article, many of which contained quotes from Charlie, Mark from the boat rental company, and a member of the Coast Guard. However, the most painful words to read were the reactions of Anna's parents. She vaguely remembered them talking to reporters during those early days, but most of that time was a blur. Anna had no idea how her parents got through it. On autopilot, she imagined.

"Bella was our youngest child. She was a bright and beautiful woman with a kind heart. We are all devastated," her father, Albert, had said.

That was an understatement.

Anna fought back the tears as a wave of emotion swept across her. She felt almost as helpless as she had four years ago.

Almost.

This time, there was a glimmer of hope that Bella could be out there somewhere.

But that hope was replaced with fear as she realized how painful it would be if this investigation turned out to be a dead end, and her dreams of seeing Bella again were dashed. Anna could very well find herself mourning Bella's death all over again.

Anna dug a small package of tissue out from the bottom of her purse and dabbed away the tears that were forming. She closed her eyes for a moment, said a prayer for guidance, then returned to the microfilm reader. She wasn't about to stop now.

Anna scanned the byline of each article, and it turned out they were all written by the same reporter, Jeremy Russo. Anna noted his name in a note on her phone, then returned the boxes of microfilm to the shelf where the librarian had taken them from. None of the details reported in the articles struck Anna as unusual, so she decided to leave. Slipping on a pair of sunglasses so that nobody could see she had been crying, she left the building.

There was still an hour before she was due to open the ice cream shop, so Anna stopped at *Cove Coffee* for an herbal tea. She was grateful to have some time to compose herself before work. Since she wasn't in the mood to make conversation after an emotional hour at the library, Anna took her tea back to her shop.

The time just before the store opened had become one of

her favorite times of the day. Since the shop didn't open until 11:00, she could either enjoy a leisurely breakfast at home on her porch, arrive early to work, or accomplish a thing or two before the workday began. The morning sun streaming through the floor-to-ceiling windows filled Anna with a deep sense of peace, which she relished particularly this morning.

Anna's thoughts drifted to Ellen's request for help the night before. Ellen would be coming by in just a few hours, and she would be expecting an answer from Anna.

Reading the articles about Bella's accident had put Anna in a different frame of mind than she had been in last night. She was reminded of the desperation that comes when certain questions remained unanswered. It had all come flooding back to her at the library. Did Anna even have it in her to revisit those days surrounding the accident as often as she would need to? And would her investigation stop her from moving on and fully embracing her new life?

She shook her head in an attempt to shake away those questions. She had already made the decision to do it. She wasn't going to turn back now just because it was getting difficult.

Anna stood abruptly and got her laptop from her office. Answering a few emails would be a good distraction. There was one from the book club that met monthly at her shop, confirming their reservation for later that evening, and another with a question about an upcoming open mic night. Before she knew it, Velma had arrived, followed shortly after by two other employees, Mary and Brian. Mary was a mom of two middle-school-aged boys, and Brian was a college student.

"There are still police officers across the street," Velma

observed.

"I imagine they'll be finishing up sometime today," Anna said.

Tuesday shaped up to be another busy day, which was just what Anna needed. The morning and afternoon flew by, and before Anna knew it, Joe had arrived for his daily scoop.

"Not that I don't love seeing you every day, Joe, but this much ice cream can't be good for your health," Anna said.

"Probably not, but you only live once."

"That's the point," Anna said. "We want your life to be a long one."

Velma appeared to be suppressing as smirk as she listened to their conversation.

"I appreciate the sentiment. I'll consider cutting down in the winter if you promise not to hassle me about it before then."

Anna chuckled. "Sounds like a plan. I do look forward to seeing you every day, so maybe I'll work on getting a healthier option in here."

While Joe was enjoying his ice cream, Anna sat on the stool next to him. "I went to the library this morning to reread some of the articles written about Bella's accident.

"I'm sorry, Anna. That must have been tough. Maybe you should have some ice cream, too," he added with a smile.

"You know, that's not a bad idea. Maybe in a little while. Anyway, the name of the reporter who covered the story was Jeremy Russo."

A smile spread across Joe's face. "Jeremy. You're in luck. He's one of the good guys."

"Do you think he'll take the time to talk with me? I haven't called him yet."

Joe nodded. "I'm sure he will."

"It sounds like you know him personally."

"I wouldn't quite say that, but over the years I've seen how he's handled sensitive stories. He's always fair and balanced, and he's respectful when talking to people in difficult circumstances. Not like some of those folks who can trample over people's feelings just to be the first to get the story. I once heard a reporter ask a grieving husband, 'How do you feel now that you've lost everything dear to you?'"

Joe appeared to be lost in thought, so Anna gave him a moment. She used the time to work up the courage to ask for the favor she hoped to obtain from him. "Do you think you could come with me when I talk to this reporter?"

Anna's question pulled Joe back to the present moment. "I don't suppose that could do any harm."

She playfully leaned against Joe. "Thanks."

After Joe left, Anna glanced at the clock and realized that it was after 4:00. Maybe Ellen had reconsidered last night's request.

However, as soon as the thought passed through Anna's head, Ellen came through the door, accompanied by a younger woman. The woman's eyes were bloodshot.

Anna took a deep breath. She hated to disappoint someone who was in so much pain.

"Hi Anna, I'd like you to meet Nicole. She's Luke's girlfriend."

Anna shook the young woman's hand.

"I was hoping you might be able to break away for an early dinner." Ellen was playing hard ball. It would be even harder to say no while they were sharing a meal.

However, Anna found herself agreeing to Ellen's request.

She grabbed her purse from the office and followed the women out the door.

CHAPTER 5

The three women settled on a sandwich shop a little further up Main Street for a light dinner. After ordering their food, they sat at a booth away from the other customers.

"Please accept my deepest condolences, Nicole," Anna said.

"Thank you. Yesterday was, by far, the worst day of my life."

"Mine, too," Ellen said.

"How's Olivia doing?" Anna asked.

"She's hanging in there. She hasn't wanted to talk about what she saw yesterday, and, frankly, I can't blame her."

"Give her some time," Anna said. "Nobody should ever have to witness what she did, especially not a sixteen-year-old."

The more they spoke about their ordeal, the more Anna could feel her defenses weakening.

"The sooner we learn who did this to Luke, the better for all of us," Ellen said.

Nicole nodded. "I don't think I slept more than two hours

last night. I've been going over in my mind every conversation I had with Luke over the past few weeks."

"That's why I asked Nicole to join us today," Ellen said. "As close as I was to my brother, I'm still twelve years older than him. He confided in me as an older sister, but Nicole probably knows things about his life that I don't. And I have to admit, I hoped that when you heard what she told me, you might be more likely to help me investigate."

Seeing the pain in the two grieving women's eyes, a pain Anna knew all too well, she knew she couldn't disappoint them. Reading the articles about Bella's death at the library this morning brought it all back. The unanswered questions. The second-guessing. Rehearsing those days in her mind and wondering "what if?" *What if we never planned that getaway weekend in Seagull Cove?* or *What if I had arrived earlier?* Anna imagined that similar questions were going through Ellen's and Nicole's minds as well. Then she thought of Joe, who had been so kind to Anna, returning to the scene of the accident with her in June and agreeing to go with her to visit with Jeremy Russo. After the kindness Joe had shown her, how could she deny *her* help to Ellen and Nicole?

Anna let out a deep breath. "I've have already decided to help you. But I don't want you to pin your hopes on me. I don't know much at all about solving murder cases. Charlie Doyle is your best bet for finding Luke's killer."

A broad smile broke on Ellen's face, which made her look five years younger than she had when she walked into *Bella's Dream* ten minutes ago.

"I completely understand," Ellen said. "And thank you."

"So, Nicole, you said that you remembered some conversations that might shed some light on what happened?"

"Possibly. You know that Luke was an insurance broker," Nicole said.

"Ellen was telling me yesterday about how he was getting his life back together after a problem that began with some prescription drugs. She and Charlie said that his future looked promising."

"Luke had a knack for sales, and he built up a healthy clientele over the past year. I helped him by taking care of some administrative tasks for him on evenings and weekends. We both hoped that eventually he could hire me full time. We made a good team. Anyway, he had this one client named Philip Pearson. Recently, there was a fire at Philip's house, and he lost everything. Philip filed an insurance claim, but soon after, the fire was verified to have been arson. The fire marshal is currently investigating Philip."

"I'm not sure I understand what that has to do with Luke," Anna said. "I get that Luke sold Philip the policy, but he couldn't possibly blame Luke for what happened."

"Philip didn't blame him for the fire, but he thought that Luke should do more to fight for him. He would call Luke every day and insist that he go to bat for him with the fire marshal. But that was way beyond Luke's pay grade. Besides, for all Luke knew, Philip was guilty."

"It clearly wasn't Luke's place to get involved," Anna said.

"That's what Luke told Philip. Repeatedly. But it didn't help that one of Luke's biggest competitors, Loni Devereaux, managed to convince Philip that if he had purchased his policy from *her*, that she would have been fighting for him. The last time Philip called Luke, he told him that if he managed to stay out of jail, he was going to work with Loni from now on."

"Is Charlie aware of this?" Anna asked.

"I told him about it when he interviewed me yesterday," Nicole said. "That's not all. Ellen, tell Anna what you told me about Nina."

"As I mentioned yesterday, Nina is Luke's ex-girlfriend. They dated during Luke's addiction years. Before he entered the rehabilitation center, Luke ended his relationship with Nina. Fortunately, Nina also entered a rehabilitation program a little less than a year ago, and is trying to get her life back on track, as well. She hoped that Luke would take her back, but he refused. He had already found Nicole."

"From what you told me yesterday, Nina didn't take it well," Anna said.

"According to Luke, she was crushed. Nina eventually stopped calling, but she made it clear that she would never give up on Luke. She believed they were meant to be."

"Luke told me that Nina had reached out to him, but he didn't tell me just how persistent she had been," Nicole said. "He probably didn't want to concern me. I'm sure it was easier to talk to Ellen about it, because she knew Nina from back in the day."

"We should speak with Nina and see if she has an alibi," Anna said.

Ellen tapped on her smartphone. "I'm pretty sure I still have Nina's address and phone number... Yes. Here it is. Maybe we could pay her a visit. I could use the excuse that I wanted to see her in person to make sure she heard about Luke."

"What about Philip?" Nicole asked.

"We'll talk to him, too, but let's start with Nina," Anna said.

"Even if she's not guilty, she may know if Luke had any enemies from the time when she knew him."

"Good idea," Ellen said.

"Let me know when you can arrange a meeting with her. Weekday mornings and afternoons are the easiest times for me to break away, since Velma works during those times."

"I'm happy to share with you anything I know about Luke's activities, but I'd rather not come with you when you talk to Nina," Nicole said.

Ellen squeezed Nicole's hand. "That's completely understandable."

"One more question," Anna said. "Did Luke have a security camera in his office?"

"There is one installed, but it never worked. Luke decided not to bother to have it repaired, because he didn't keep anything of value in there and didn't see the need to," Nicole said.

The three women exchanged phone numbers and finished their sandwiches before leaving the restaurant.

By the time Anna returned to *Bella's Dream*, her evening shift employees had arrived. Emily, another college student, along with Trish and Jack, had things under control. Anna hopped behind the counter to help them with the after-dinner rush, and before she knew it, it was closing time.

When Casper came for his nightly visit, Anna was convinced that he still seemed downcast. However, he did manage to finish all his chicken this time.

Anna cleaned Casper's bowl, locked the building, and was about to head home when she heard a whistle. She looked in the direction of the sound, and it was Joe leaning against the railing on his small porch. She walked toward him and stood beneath the porch.

"It's a beautiful night," she said.

"That it is. I happened to see Jeremy Russo earlier this evening. He was poking around across the street asking questions about Luke's death. I took the liberty of telling him that you wanted to pick his brain, and he said he'd be in the newsroom tomorrow morning."

"That's great news! Thanks Joe."

"How about if we meet in front of *Bella's Dream* at 9:30?"

"Perfect. I'll see you then."

July was shaping up to be a busy month.

Before heading home for the night, Anna decided to take a walk along the beach to wind down. The population of Seagull Cove swelled during the summer months due to tourists and seasonal residents, who returned in droves once the warmer weather came. Many of them seemed to be out and about tonight. Anna passed the cove and continued to Mile Long Beach. She inhaled deeply, taking in the fresh night air.

Just as Anna was about to turn around and head home, a man called out from the front porch of one of the large Victorian homes across the street from the beach, "Anna, is that you?"

Anna followed the voice to a man sitting in a white wooden rocker beneath a porchlight. It was Wanda's husband.

"Hi, Daniel." There was something vaguely familiar about the house. She had the feeling she had been in there before, but she couldn't remember when.

"Out for a walk after work?" Daniel asked in a friendly voice.

"It's a beautiful night for it. The summer is passing by much too quickly."

"Well, don't forget to enjoy it before the cold and snow come along."

"You're right," Anna said. "I was just thinking that I need to take some time off." If she could find the time, that is. She had a lot on her plate at the moment.

"Sounds like a wise plan."

Anna had so many questions for Daniel. Had Wanda shared this beautiful home with him? Why was she living in a little cottage next to Anna when her husband lived here? But she didn't dare ask. Instead, she suppressed the urge to be nosy. "You have the right idea, Daniel. I think I'll get home so I can do what you're doing and sit on my front porch."

Daniel smiled. "I highly recommend it. It's a wonderful way to pass an evening as beautiful as tonight."

CHAPTER 6

The following morning, Anna's phone pinged with a text from Ellen.

Nina said we could come by any time before 3:00. How about 2:00?

That works for me.

Great. She lives fifteen minutes away. I'll pick you up at 1:45 at Bella's Dream.

Anna tossed her phone back on the table, waved at Wanda, who was weeding her garden next door, and proceeded to do some weeding of her own.

When Anna arrived at *Bella's Dream* at 9:30 to meet Joe, he was already waiting for her with two iced coffees in hand. She took a deep breath and tried to mentally prepare herself for her conversation with Jeremy Russo.

"Thanks, Joe," she said as he handed her one of the iced coffees.

They walked a quarter of a mile to the old grey-shingled building located at the top of Main Street, which housed the

Seagull Cove Chronicle. Anna followed Joe up the rickety wooden staircase that led to the third floor newsroom. The room's large windows framed a Norman Rockwell-type view of Main Street.

The newspaper appeared to be a small operation. The newsroom contained six computer stations and two offices with floor-to-ceiling windows on the left side of the room. A man with dark wavy hair, wearing black pleated pants and a white polo shirt motioned for them to wait a second when they entered the room. The man, who looked to be about Anna's age, was talking on his cell phone.

Joe waved at him.

Less than a minute later, he disconnected the call and came over to greet them.

"Hi, Joe, it's great to see you. How is retirement treating you?"

Joe smirked at Anna. "It was going just ducky until Anna here dragged me out kicking and screaming to work on Marcus Grady's murder investigation."

Jeremy's eyes widened. "Oh, you're *that* Anna. I didn't make the connection. It looks like the ice cream business is going well."

Did this guy know everything that happened in Seagull Cove?

"Business has been great since we solved that case."

"I have to admit, I was impressed," Jeremy said with a smile. He had an easy smile that put Anna at ease. She imagined that it came in handy as a reporter. He was probably very good at getting people to open up.

"You must be a persuasive woman if you convinced Old Joe Wiggins to take on another case. I'm glad everything worked out." His dark eyes seemed to look right through Anna, and she wasn't sure if she liked the feeling.

"Joe has a huge heart," Anna said.

"Now, don't go around saying that. I just didn't want my favorite ice cream shop to close," Joe teased.

Jeremy winked at Anna. "Despite what Joe would like people to believe, those of us who have known him for a while know that he's not that shallow." His gaze lingered on Anna. "Joe must like you."

"I'm glad to be able to connect the two of you," Joe continued. "Anna is new in town."

"What brought you to Seagull Cove?" Jeremy asked. "There are plenty of towns where one could open an ice cream shop."

Anna took a few minutes to explain how her family had vacationed here each summer while she was growing up, and that she and her siblings had continued the tradition into their adult life. She briefly told him about the ice cream shop in Boston that she and Bella used to visit on Friday afternoons, and how Bella had often fantasized about opening an ice cream shop that would be a community hub. Four years after Bella's accident, Anna realized she needed a change, so she decided to open *Bella's Dream*. "Some of my happiest memories are in Seagull Cove, so it seemed like the perfect place to relocate."

"I was wondering why you named your shop *Bella's Dream*. That makes perfect sense. In fact, it's the perfect name. Seagull Cove could use a business like yours. I'm sorry I haven't come by yet to check it out. It's been a busy summer."

"Be sure to order a banana split. It's Anna's signature dessert," Joe said.

Jeremy smiled. "I'm a straight up hot fudge sundae kind of guy."

"We have those, too," Anna said.

Jeremy's expression grew serious. "I know you didn't come by to discuss ice cream." He accompanied them into a small conference room at the front of the newsroom, where Anna and Joe sat across from Jeremy. "Now that I see you, I vaguely remember you from when I covered Bella's accident. I remember your parents vividly. They were very gracious when I interviewed them. I hope they are doing well."

"It's still very difficult. Sometimes if feels like yesterday that we lost her, and other days, it seems like we've lived a lifetime without her."

"Joe tells me that you wanted to talk about the articles I wrote. Was there something specific you wanted to know?"

Anna glanced at Joe, and he gave her an encouraging nod.

"I'm exploring the possibility that my sister didn't actually die in that boating accident."

Jeremy's eyes widened. "I remember that they never found her body, but if she didn't die, don't you think she would have contacted you by now?"

"There are a lot of questions I can't answer, and that's one of them," Anna said.

"I don't understand. What makes you think she could still be alive?"

"It all started on the day of my grand opening. There is a framed photo of Bella hanging in my ice cream shop. When Joe saw it for the first time, he told me that he thought he saw that same woman across the street earlier that day, peering into my shop."

Jeremy shifted his gaze to Joe. "Are you sure?"

Joe shook his head. "I can't be positive. I told Anna that."

"But still, Joe has sharp observation skills," Jeremy said.

"A couple of weeks after that, Joe and I rented a boat and took it to the scene of the boating accident. We both agreed that if Bella had wanted to stage her death, that would have been the perfect place to do it."

Jeremy leaned back in his chair, allowing the front legs to lift off the ground, and looked intently at Anna. "I suppose you could be right. In theory. But why would your sister do something like that? Did Bella have a past that she might need to escape from?"

"No. At least, not that I know of," Anna said. "And we were very close."

"If Bella staged her own death, that would have been a dramatic move that would change her life forever, not to mention the lives of all those who loved her. Didn't she have a fiancé?"

"Bella and Grayson weren't engaged, although they were close to it. I don't know why she would have left everything and everyone she loved behind to start a new life. It sounds crazy even saying it out loud. Those are more questions that I don't have answers to," Anna said. "I do realize that I might be on a wild goose chase, but think of it from my perspective. If there is even the slightest chance that my sister could be alive, I have to see this through."

"I guess I can understand where you're coming from. So, you're wondering if I noticed anything while I was covering the story that would indicate she could still be alive," Jeremy observed.

"That's correct. Was there anything at all you noticed that could indicate that my sister's boating accident was staged?"

Jeremy ran a tan hand through his thick dark hair. "The thought never even occurred to me, Anna. Before you came today, I reread my articles to refresh my memory. As far as I was concerned, I was covering a tragic fatal accident. The police never investigated for foul play, and I didn't notice anything that appeared inconsistent with an accident. But I suppose I didn't see anything that proved beyond a shadow of a doubt that she died, either."

Anna wasn't sure what she was hoping that Jeremy would say, but that was an anticlimactic conversation.

"You know the details surrounding Bella's accident as well as anyone," Anna said. "Would it be okay if I contacted you as another sounding board if I should discover anything?"

"Of course." Jeremy handed Anna his card. "My cell phone number is on there. Call me any time. I sincerely hope that you are right, Anna, but I'm not going to lie. The chances seem slim."

"I understand. One more thing," Anna said. "I will keep you posted on my findings as long as you promise that it's off the record. If my sister *is* alive, there is a reason why she wants the world to believe she died in that accident."

"Of course," Jeremy said. "I'll make a deal with you. I'll support you in any way I can if you promise that, if Bella is alive, you will encourage her to share her story with me. If and when she is ready, that is."

That seemed fair. Anna could only hope that she would find herself in that position. "You've got a deal. Thank you for your time, Jeremy."

Anna and Joe headed back to *Bella's Dream*. "How do you feel?" Joe asked, after a few minutes of walking in silence.

"I guess my feelings are mixed. I suppose I was hoping that

once I told Jeremy about my suspicions, that he might think of a lead where I could begin my investigation. You know, some odd fact or clue that I could pursue. But that was probably a long shot. I do appreciate his discretion and his willingness to help if he can. I'm glad I reached out to him. Thanks for coming with me, Joe."

"Jeremy is a good man. You can trust him. Do you know what your next step is going to be?"

"If Bella is alive, she obviously believes that it's better for everyone to think she is dead. Maybe the best route to take is not to try to figure out *if* she staged her death, but rather *why*? If Bella is alive, figuring out why she faked her death might answer more questions."

"Good thinking," Joe said.

Anna felt a twinge of pride at receiving a compliment from a real-life retired private investigator.

"When I moved to Seagull Cove, I put all of the paperwork related to our counseling practice in my attic. I also have a lot of Bella's personal financial records up there, since I was the one who closed out her accounts. The first thing I'm going to do is scour all those documents to look for anything out of the ordinary that I may have missed. You know, something that might reveal any strange behavior."

"I think that's a logical place to start," Joe said. "Keep me posted."

CHAPTER 7

When Anna and Joe had reached *Bella's Dream*, Joe went upstairs to his apartment, and Anna continued walking toward the cove. She needed to clear her mind and refocus on the day ahead after her conversation with Jeremy Russo.

By the time she arrived at work, Velma had already opened the shop, and Mary and Kathy, the other two staff members who were scheduled to work the first shift on Wednesday, had just arrived. Kathy was a retired executive assistant for a local company who only worked a few days a week, just to get out of the house.

It was another sunny July morning, and the hot weather brought in a steady stream of customers looking to escape the sun and cool off with an ice cream. Anna periodically hopped behind the counter when the line got long. The hours flew by, and before Anna knew it, Ellen had arrived to take her to Nina's for their meeting at 2:00.

Anna hopped into Ellen's car, and they drove to Beverly, the town where Nina lived. They climbed the stairs to the third-floor walkup, and Ellen knocked on an old wooden door. A tall, thin woman with straight brown hair greeted them. She wore a black polo shirt that was embroidered with the name "Pete's Pub."

"Come in," she said, as she stepped back to allow them to enter. "Can I get you something to drink?"

"No, thanks," Ellen said.

Anna shook her head. "No, thank you."

The two women sat on a worn-out grey sofa while their hostess sat across from them on a tan recliner.

"I know from our phone conversation that you already heard about Luke's death," Ellen said.

Tears spilled from Nina's eyes as she nodded. She took a tissue from a box on the side table next to the recliner and patted her eyes. "I saw it on the news. I'm so sorry, Ellen. I hope you know that I never stopped caring about Luke."

"I am in the process of notifying his friends. I was hoping to reach you before you heard about it on the news."

"Thanks, Ellen. I really do appreciate that. I was devastated when I heard. The news story played on the TV at the bar in the restaurant where I work. I don't know where I found the strength to finish my shift."

"I'm sorry you had to hear the news that way. By the way, this is my friend, Anna. She's been a great source of support for me and offered to come with me today."

"Hi, Anna. Did you know Luke?"

"Unfortunately, I didn't. But from all the wonderful things that I've heard from Olivia and Ellen, it sounds like he was a good man."

Anna spotted a half-empty bottle of brandy on the floor next to Nina's recliner.

"Luke was the best thing that ever happened to me," Nina said.

"I understand that you recently reached out to Luke to reconnect," Ellen said.

"I did. We had coffee together. I wanted to thank him for being the catalyst for my getting clean. It took me a little longer than it took Luke to get on the right path, but I eventually checked myself into the same rehabilitation center that Luke did, and I've been clean ever since. When I saw Luke trying to turn his life around, something clicked. I figured that if Luke could do it, then I could, too."

Ellen glanced at the half empty liquor bottle.

"I didn't say I was perfect," Nina said, a couple of octaves louder than she had been speaking, "but I'm not doing drugs anymore." Nina closed her eyes and took a deep breath. "I'm sorry for snapping. It's been a long day, and it's only half over. When I heard the news of Luke's death on Monday night, I came home and had a few drinks. When I woke up the next morning, I realized that that's not what Luke would have wanted me to do. But, as I said, I'm not perfect. It was a lot to deal with."

Ellen looked as if she, too, might have been on the verge of tears, so Anna took over. "I recently opened an ice cream shop in Seagull Cove. I love not having to start work until 11:00 in the morning. I'm becoming quite the night owl. I find it's hard to go right to sleep when I close the shop, so I usually take a walk or sit on my front porch to unwind."

"I know what you mean," Nina said. "By the time I get home it's close to midnight."

Ellen furrowed her brow as she listened to Anna, but she didn't interrupt.

"Me, too. Sometimes I don't wake up until 10:00," Nina said.

Understanding dawned on Ellen's face.

Ellen seemed to get that Anna was trying to determine whether Nina had an alibi for Monday morning, when Luke was killed.

"Were you sleeping on the morning when Luke passed away?" Anna asked.

"I work late every weekend, so on Monday mornings I always sleep in. This week was no exception."

"Ellen tells me that you once knew Luke quite well. Do you have any idea who would have wanted to hurt Luke?"

"We haven't had a lot of contact in the last year." Nina narrowed her eyes. "Besides Nicole, I don't know who is in his life right now."

"I was thinking more along the lines of someone from when *you* knew him," Anna clarified.

"I don't know a lot about that time in his life," Ellen added. "Did he have any enemies that you know about?"

Nina ran her hand through her straight brown hair. "We kept to ourselves a lot back then. We only had a small group of friends. I can't think of anyone who didn't like Luke. It must have been someone he met after we broke up. What about his new girlfriend, Nicole?"

Ellen's eyes flew wide open. Although Ellen appeared shocked that Nina would suggest such a thing, Anna was actually glad that she had. She was planning to ask Ellen what she knew about their relationship the next time they were alone. They couldn't leave any stone unturned.

"Nicole would never hurt Luke. She loved him," Ellen said. "Besides, she was out to breakfast with some of her coworkers at a restaurant near her office in Gloucester at the time Luke was killed. She couldn't have done it. There are several people who could give her an alibi."

Anna was relieved to hear that. Ellen was obviously fond of Nicole, and it would have been traumatic for her and the rest of her family if Nicole had turned out to be Luke's killer.

Nina looked toward the ground. "I'm glad to hear that. You know, there *is* one person who comes to mind from Luke's distant past, before I knew him. Do you remember that night we came to Seagull Cove and Luke asked you for money?"

"There were a number of times that happened," Ellen said.

"But there was only *one* time when I was with him. I was waiting in the car this time."

Ellen nodded. "I do remember. Luke asked me and my husband for some cash, but we refused. We gave him some food, but we wouldn't give him any money. He didn't talk to us for months after that."

"After he visited you that night, he paid his friend, Wil, a visit. Luke asked him for money, but he also refused, so we..." Nina's voice trailed off.

Anna guessed what she was getting at. "You stole money from Wil?"

Nina nodded. "Luke was furious with him for refusing to help us. He pretended to go to the bathroom, but instead he sneaked into the coat closet, pulled Wil's wallet from his coat pocket, and took all the cash out of it. He also took a credit card, and we charged a bunch of things to it. I'm ashamed to say that we would have spent more, but Wil canceled the credit card the following day."

"He must have figured out that it was Luke who stole it," Anna said.

"Oh, he definitely figured it out. The following evening, Luke and I heard a loud knock on the door, and when Luke answered it, Wil came unglued. Luke asked me to leave for a little while, so I went for a walk. I'm sure Luke denied everything to Wil's face, but Wil obviously knew better, or he wouldn't have come."

"Did Luke ever repay Wil for the money he stole?" Ellen asked.

"Not that I know of."

"But still," Anna said. "That had to be a year-and-a-half ago."

"That's about right," Nina said.

"So, why would Wil wait a year-and-a-half and then kill Luke over an old grudge? That doesn't seem like a very strong motive to me," Anna said.

"That's a good point," Ellen said.

Since Nina couldn't help them any further, they thanked her for her time and left.

"Do you think Nina killed Luke?" Ellen asked as they drove back to Seagull Cove.

"She said that she slept in on Monday morning, but I doubt she could prove that. Although she *did* seem genuinely upset about Luke's passing."

"She could have been faking it," Ellen said. "Maybe she killed him out of jealousy when she realized that he wouldn't get back together with her, even after she cleaned her life up."

"It's possible. I don't think she was faking her grief, but that doesn't necessarily mean she's innocent," Anna said. "And even though Wil isn't a very strong suspect, I think it's probably worth having a conversation with him. Did they ever make up after Luke got clean?"

"It took a little time, but they did eventually become friends again," Ellen said.

Ellen appeared to be lost in thought as she drove in silence.

"What are you thinking about?" Anna finally asked.

"I'm thinking about Wil and Luke. It's strange, because Wil forgave Luke after he cleaned up his life and they became friends again, but a couple of weeks ago, I asked Luke to invite Wil to my house for Sunday dinner, and he told me they had had a falling out. He wouldn't say any more than that, but there was a pained expression on Luke's face when I brought up Wil."

"We definitely need to talk to him then, so we can find out what happened. Plus, since Wil and Luke had been friends for a long time, he might be able to point us in the right direction. We should talk to Philip, too."

"How about if I tell Philip that I am notifying all of Luke's clients in person about his death? I'm sure Nicole could find his contact information in Luke's files. That way, we could pay him a surprise visit."

"That could work. Since he doesn't know that *you* know about the fire, he would probably believe that you think he's still a client. You could say that you're paying all of Luke's business contacts a courtesy call."

"I'll talk to Nicole and get back to you," Ellen said as she parked in front of *Bella's Dream*.

Anna exited Ellen's car just as Joe was coming in for his daily scoop. He looked at Ellen in the driver's seat, then back at Anna.

Shoot. Joe was bound to deduce that Anna was helping Ellen look for Luke's killer.

CHAPTER 8

*J*oe stopped and waited for Anna before entering *Bella's Dream*. He smirked as he held open the door.

"Wasn't that Olivia's mother?" he asked, taking his usual stool at the ice cream counter.

Anna placed a scoop of chocolate chip ice cream and a glass of water in front of him while Velma rang up his order.

"It was. We've become friends since her brother passed away. Having both lost a sibling, we have a lot in common."

"I see," Joe said. "So, having this tragedy in common, combined with your reputation as the town's amateur sleuth, hasn't inspired her to ask you for any favors that involve an investigation, have they?"

"I think you overestimate my reputation," Anna said, avoiding the question. Out of the corner of her eye, she noticed that the one of the trash receptacles in the dining room was overflowing. She nodded in the direction of the overflowing trash. "I'd better take care of that."

"I'll get the other one," Brian said, grabbing the bag in the other receptacle and following Anna out to the trash dumpster.

But Anna knew that her narrow escape wouldn't buy her much time. Joe was bound to realize that she hadn't answered his question. Anna made a mental note to schedule any sleuthing-related activities either before or after Joe came in for his mid-afternoon ice cream break.

When Anna and Brian returned from emptying the trash, Joe was talking with a little boy who had come in with his parents and were sitting at a bistro table near one of the front windows.

A few minutes later, Anna went back into her office. She had left her cell phone on her desk, and when she picked it up there was a voicemail from Ellen asking Anna to call her back. Anna stepped outside and sat on the bench out front while she returned the call.

"Hi Anna," Ellen answered. "I spoke with Nicole. She's taking a few days off, so she was at home and was able to get me Philip's contact information right away. I have the address of the house that he is renting. What do you say we pop in on him and pay him a surprise visit? Nicole said he owns a startup and works from home, so I think we could go anytime."

"That sounds like a good idea. Are you free now? Velma is here until 5:00, so it's a good time for me to leave."

"I don't have to pick the kids up from camp for another two hours. I'll be by to pick you up in a few minutes," Ellen said.

Anna arranged to meet Ellen up the street, so that Joe

wouldn't see her getting into Ellen's car again. Within ten minutes, they were zipping across town to Philip's rental house.

They pulled up to a small white house not too far from the highway and rang the doorbell.

A man who looked to be in his mid-thirties with wavy brown hair, wearing blue jeans and a black untucked polo, answered the door. There was a laptop sitting on the couch and papers strewn all around.

"Well, hello there, ladies. How can I help you?"

"Are you Philip Pearson?" Ellen asked.

He looked behind them, apparently to see if they were alone, before responding. "I am. Who's asking?"

"My name is Ellen Montgomery, and this is my friend, Anna. I'm afraid we have some unfortunate news to share with you. Would it be possible for us to come inside and talk?"

"There's no news you could possibly bring that could make my life any worse than it is now. My house recently burned down, and my girlfriend broke up with me."

"I'm sorry to hear that," Ellen said. "But I'm quite certain we have the right person."

Philip stepped aside so the women could enter. He stacked the papers that were strewn about on his couch, then motioned for them to sit on the loveseat across from him. "So, what tragic news have you come to deliver?"

"My brother was Luke Carter. I believe he was your insurance agent."

Philip smiled, but his eyes contained more contempt than kindness. "*Was* is the operative word. No offense to your brother, but that dude didn't do me any favors as my agent. The fire marshal is trying to pin the fire at my house on me, as if I'd burn down my own house just for some insurance money. Your brother won't even go to bat for me. He was very attentive while he was trying to sell me a policy, but now that I need him, he's nowhere to be found. What did he do, send you here to apologize?"

Ellen clenched her fists and took a breath. Either Philip was the most insensitive person in Seagull Cove, or he hadn't yet heard about Luke's death.

Anna chose to give him the benefit of the doubt. They wouldn't get any information out of him if Ellen told him off, so she stepped in.

"We're not here to talk about your insurance claim," Anna said. "Your name was in Luke's business contacts, so this is a courtesy call. We came to let you know that Luke passed away and will no longer be able to service your insurance needs."

Philip smirked. "Well, hopefully there was a big life insurance policy."

Ellen looked fit to be tied, and Anna couldn't blame her. She put her hand on Ellen's forearm as a show of support and then tried another approach.

"Look, Philip, Ellen is here out of courtesy. She just lost her brother, so the least you could do is be a little sensitive."

"No offense to you, Ellen. You seem like a nice lady. I suppose that last comment was uncalled for. But your brother really left me in a bind. He convinced me to invest in a hefty insurance policy, and then just when I need it, I get grief from the fire marshal. A good agent would fight for me. That's what Loni Devereaux says, anyway. She's been calling me every week since the fire. I should have gone with her from the beginning."

"It sounds like you're pretty angry at Luke," Anna said.

"You bet."

"Mad enough to kill him?"

Philip stared at Anna, stunned. The man was finally speechless.

His eyes widened as he apparently processed the accusation. "Whoa, wait a minute. I didn't kill anybody!"

"You certainly seem mad enough to kill him. We came here to inform you that your insurance agent is no longer alive, and you respond with insults. You seem pretty angry to me. Perhaps even angry enough to kill."

"The two of you need to leave right now. How dare you come into my home and accuse me of murder!"

Philip did have a point. They *were* in his home. But when Anna saw the expression on Ellen's face after Philip insulted Luke, she thought of how she would feel if someone had insulted Bella two days after her death.

Anna and Ellen stood to leave. "We'll be going. But I'm sure the police will be by to question you, since you obviously have a motive for murder. For your sake, I hope you have an alibi."

"When was he murdered?"

"Monday morning about 8:00."

"I was having breakfast with my buddy, Tim. Besides, what reason would I have for killing Luke? It's not like it would solve any of my problems," he said as he ushered them out the door.

"Revenge," Ellen said under her breath after Philip slammed the door behind them.

"Are you okay?" Anna asked. "I'm sorry he was such an insensitive jerk."

"I'll get over it. The only reason I didn't tell him off and storm out was because I want to get to the bottom of what happened to my brother." Ellen wiped a tear that threatened to fall from her eye. "But that was tough to sit through."

"I'd say Philip is definitely a strong suspect," Anna said when they got in the car. "His alibi is weak, and he is clearly harboring a boatload of resentment toward your brother."

"I think we should talk to Nicole again and find out more about what happened. Do you have time to stop by her house?" Ellen asked.

Anna glanced at the time on Ellen's dashboard. "I need to make a quick stop at *The Book Cove,* and then I really should get back to work. It's been busy all day, so I'm expecting another rush of customers. Do you think Nicole could come by *Bella's Dream* so we could talk there? We can go into my office for privacy. That way, if my employees need me, I'll be right there."

"I don't see why not. I want to go home and check on my kids, anyway. I'll call Nicole from my house."

"Sounds great. Come anytime. I'll be there until 10:00 tonight."

Anna scurried over to *The Book Cove* hoping to find Ruthie Valentino, the shop's owner. She smiled when she spotted Ruthie rearranging the display window.

Anna knocked on the glass and motioned for Ruthie to come out so she could ask her something. Anna was on a mission, and she was determined not to leave without accomplishing it.

"Hi, Anna. It's great to see you. Are you here for another gardening book?"

"Nope. But the one I bought a couple of months ago has been tremendously helpful." Anna took out her phone and showed Ruthie the photos of her English garden. "Of course, I owe a lot of gratitude to my neighbor, Wanda. Without her help, I'd still be studying my book and wondering where I should start."

"It looks beautiful. Thank you for showing me. It's always nice to learn when my books helped someone to do something so amazing."

"I would love to have you over to see it in person. Perhaps you, me, Rosie, and Sonja could have lunch at my house one day soon." Rosie was the proprietor of the *Inn at Seagull Cove*, and Sonja owned *Cove Coffee*.

"I would love that. It will be a good incentive to take a couple of hours off from work."

"Great, I will email everyone and arrange it for some time next month." Anna hoped by then that Luke's killer would be behind bars, and she wouldn't be taking time off to investigate. "But that's not why I came. I wanted to talk to you about your poetry. I loved that poem you shared with me about a seaside cottage."

"Thank you. I do scribble some poetry here and there, but I don't often share my work with anyone. I just thought it might inspire you since you had just bought your own cottage."

"It totally did. And I think your no-share policy needs to change."

A voice came from behind Anna. "I totally agree. Ruthie's poetry is amazing. I've been telling her that she should publish it, but she won't hear of it."

Anna turned around to find a young man wearing a red t-shirt with the bookstore's logo embroidered on the front.

"I'm an English Literature major, and her stuff is better than some of the junk we have to read in class. But good luck convincing Ruthie of that."

"I have a proposal that might be a nice middle ground," Anna said. "I'm having my first open mic night at *Bella's Dream* on Thursday. I'd like for you to be the first person to take the stage."

Ruthie shook her head in dismay. "Oh, no you don't. How is that middle ground? I'd rather publish my poems than stand in front of all those people and read them."

"It's only my first open mic night, so I doubt there will be *that* many people. Besides, at least you will see right away whether people like your poems. If they like them as much as I think they will, it might give you the confidence to publish them."

"I loathe speaking in front of people. No way. Besides, I have to work Thursday night."

"I'll cover for you," the young man said.

"There. Now you have no excuses. I'm not going to take 'no' for an answer. This will be good for you."

Ruthie glanced at Anna, then at her employee. "I don't think so."

"Just promise you'll think about it."

"We'll convince her to do it," the young man said. "Plan on Ruthie being there."

"I hate you guys," Ruthie said.

"We love you, too," the young man said.

Anna smiled at Ruthie. "You're going to be great. You can do this."

Ruthie didn't look at all convinced. Anna left with a twinge of guilt at bringing so much anxiety to a friend she only recently met. Even though it was for Ruthie's own good, tough love was, well… tough.

CHAPTER 9

Shortly after Anna returned to work, Ellen texted her to say she and Nicole would be coming by later to talk. The women arrived a couple of hours later, and since Anna's employees had the ice cream line under control, the three women decided to go for a stroll along the beach. They walked past the cove and down to Mile Long Beach. Although it was early evening, the beach was still filled with a people enjoying the surf and sand.

"Summer was Luke's favorite season," Ellen said. "He spent every spare moment either at the beach or on the water."

"Bella loved the summer, too," Anna said. "I think of her every time I come to the beach."

Anna and Ellen filled Nicole in on their conversations with both Nina and Philip, although they left out the part about Nina suggesting that Nicole murdered Luke.

"Philip seemed thoroughly convinced that Luke should have been advocating for him after his house burned down," Anna said. "He claimed that his current agent, Loni Devereaux, is calling weekly with updates. We were hoping that you might know whether there was any legitimacy to Philip's complaints."

Nicole ran a hand through her shoulder length blond hair. "I don't think so. Philip was one of Luke's first clients, so I didn't meet him until after the fire. But I was already working for Luke when Philip's home burned down. Luke helped him to file a claim, even though that's not part of his job, but once it was discovered that the cause of the fire was arson, there was nothing much Luke could do. Philip had to wait for the state fire marshal to finish his investigation and present his findings. Philip was livid that Luke wasn't more involved and really let Luke have it. And then when he found out that Luke was new to the business, things got even worse. Philip started insisting that Luke didn't know how to take care of his clients properly. Loni didn't exactly help the matter. That woman was determined to make Luke look bad. She even started badmouthing him to potential clients after the fire. She was thrilled to have something to tarnish Luke's reputation with."

"Do you think Loni would have killed Luke to eliminate the competition?" Anna asked.

"I mean, who does that?" Nicole asked. "It's a cutthroat business, and she's been in it a lot longer than Luke was. I can't imagine that she'd go around killing any insurance agent who was giving her a little competition."

"That's a good point," Ellen said. "But I still think we should talk to her. It may be a weak motive, but it's still a motive, and we don't have many strong suspects."

"Fair enough," Anna said. "She may know if Luke had any other clients who we should be looking at."

"Besides Loni, who else do you plan to talk to?" Nicole asked.

"Just Wil," Ellen said. "Nina told us that she and Luke stole money from him. It was a while back and they did reconcile after that, but something happened between them a couple of weeks ago."

"What do you mean?" Nicole asked. "Luke didn't mention that to me. But he *did* say that Wil and his ex-wife got back together, so maybe Wil has just been busy."

"Luke told me about their reconciliation. That's wonderful news! I never understood why Wil and Danielle separated to begin with. They were so good together."

"They broke up just before I met Luke, so I never met Danielle," Nicole said. "But Luke seemed happy about the reconciliation." Nicole furrowed her brow.

"What is it? Did you think of something important?" Anna asked.

"I don't know if it's important, but I just remembered that Luke told me that he wanted to talk to me about something to do with Wil, but we never got the chance. He said that there was something he wanted me to know and that he would tell me the next time we got together. This was on Sunday night, the night before his death. With everything that happened, it slipped my mind. Maybe he was going to tell me what happened between them."

"I got the impression it was significant, because when I asked Luke to invite Wil to Sunday dinner a couple of weeks ago, he specifically told me that something had happened between them and that he was giving Wil some space," Ellen said. "I can't imagine that it was something that would be a motive for murder, but I don't think we should leave any stone left unturned."

"Agreed," Nicole said. "That sounds like a solid next step.

Keep me posted."

After their walk, Anna returned to *Bella's Dream*. There were still a couple of hours before closing time. It was a warm evening, so Main Street was bustling with tourists and summer residents. Anna happily spent the remainder of the night assisting her employees behind the counter and greeting customers. When it was time to leave, she was bone tired. It had been a long day.

She fed Casper his nightly meal and dragged herself home.

Despite her exhaustion, Anna's mind was restless as she thought about her conversation with Jeremy. She made herself some black tea to give herself a boost of energy and decided that it was as good a time as any to start looking through Bella's old financial records.

Anna yanked down the wooden staircase from the ceiling in her bedroom, which gave access to the attic, and climbed up. She brought down all the boxes that contained old paperwork connected to Bella, including her personal files and Bella's files from the counseling practice.

She piled the four boxes by the coffee table in her living room and started with the one that was labeled "Receipts and Statements." Although it had been Anna who handled the paperwork involved with Bella's death, those early months were a blur. She vaguely remembered obtaining the death certificate and closing out Bella's accounts. At the time, there was no reason to examine Bella's paperwork for anything suspicious. It had all been so painfully simple - the letter addressed "To Whom it May Concern" stating that Isabel McBride had died in a boating accident, the enclosed death certificate. It was all cut and dry. No questions asked by the creditors or by Anna. Until recently.

First, Anna perused her sister's bank statements. Her checking account looked normal. Bella had had a few thousand dollars in the account when she died. There was no balance in her savings account, which hadn't surprised Anna. They had invested a lot of money in their practice during the first year, and Anna knew that Bella had needed to pay off some debt and take care of some delayed expenses, such as dental work, once the practice started doing well.

Next, Anna opened the file that contained the statements from Bella's retirement account. There had been nothing in it at the time of her death, because she closed it out to pay off the remaining debt she had acquired during that first lean year of the practice. Anna remembered that their accountant had advised against it, but Anna didn't question Bella's final decision to do it. Anna had barely been able to make ends meet, so she understood why her sister had come to the decision that she had.

Anna dug back a few months into the statements from the retirement account and was surprised to see that before she closed it out, Bella had nearly $75,000 in her retirement account.

How much credit card debt did Bella have?

Anna went back to Bella's credit card statements to find out. In the months before closing out her retirement account, Bella hadn't been carrying much of a balance at all. Only a few hundred dollars, which she paid off each month.

So, what happened to the $75,000 that Bella withdrew from her retirement account?

Anna went back even further, checking every statement from Bella's two credit card accounts, which went back seven years, and discovered that Bella had never carried a significant balance. During their first year of the practice, Bella had accumulated a few thousand dollars' worth of debt, but she paid that off six months later.

This didn't make any sense. Why did Bella lie about being in debt? And more importantly, where did that $75,000 from her 401k go?

Anna decided to scour Bella's savings account. She had only looked at the most recent statement to determine the balance, but with her new discovery, she took a closer look.

She couldn't believe her eyes.

A month before Bella's accident, she had also withdrawn just over $10,000 from her savings account. That made a total of $85,000 in withdrawals in the months before her accident.

Anna leaned back on her couch and stared at the wall in shock. She couldn't believe that she had never examined her sister's records more closely. But then again, why would she? She had no reason to doubt anything Bella told her regarding her personal finances. As far as Anna knew, Bella had no reason to lie. Anna hadn't even asked about the retirement account. It was Bella who volunteered the information.

Anna's theory about Bella staging her own death for some mysterious reason was no longer looking so farfetched. If Anna's theory was correct, Bella would have needed as much money as she could get her hands on to start over. Anna thought back to when Bella told her about closing out her 401k. Did her sister give Anna this unsolicited information so that, after Bella's supposed death, Anna wouldn't wonder the exact thing that she was wondering now?

The more Anna turned the facts over in her mind, the stronger a possibility it seemed.

CHAPTER 10

It was well after midnight before Anna finally managed to fall asleep.

On Thursday morning, her first thought was about all the money Bella had withdrawn from her accounts in the months that preceded her death. If Bella had truly died in that accident, where did all that money go?

As she lay in bed, Anna considered telling her parents what she had discovered, but she quickly decided against it. She also considered confiding in Albie, but she didn't want her big brother breathing down her neck as she searched for answers.

Before she finally dragged herself out of bed at 9:00, Anna had determined that the only people she could tell would be Joe Wiggins and possibly Jeremy Russo. At least for now.

Anna took a quick shower, changed into black capris and her blue work polo, and brought a bowl of cereal and her largest mug filled with extra strong coffee onto the front porch. Admiring her little garden and cozy front porch brought her some peace. With so many unanswered questions swirling around in her mind, the one thing Anna did know was that she was exactly where she should be – on the front porch of her cottage in Seagull Cove overlooking her colorful garden and preparing to head to *Bella's Dream*.

Despite her sister's tragedy, Seagull Cove was still her happy place.

After she finished breakfast and a second mug of coffee, Anna watered the potted herbs on her porch, the purple English lavender and yellow black-eyed susans in her barn-red pony cart on the front lawn, and the plants and flowers in her mini garden in front of the house.

As she wrapped up the hose, Anna noticed out of the corner of her eye that Wanda was waving from her yard.

"Good morning, Wanda."

"It looked like you were lost in thought."

Anna smiled. "I guess I was. I was thinking about my sister."

Wanda's expression grew sympathetic. "The one you named the ice cream shop after."

"Yes. Bella. She's been on my mind a lot lately." Anna was tempted to tell Wanda what she had discovered the night before. She found herself in the mood to talk about it, and she had the feeling that Wanda could keep a secret. But she held back. She still didn't know Wanda that well, so she didn't want to overshare.

Wanda's expression grew solemn. "I'll leave you with your memories of your loved one," she said, and continued to water her garden.

Anna arrived at *Bella's Dream* at the same time as Velma, Emily, Alex, and Jack. She smiled as Jack, a high school student, listened intently to Alex as Alex told him about how he chose his college and why he decided to major in Business. Alex was always patient with Jack's questions, and he seemed to be a good influence on Jack, so Anna did her best to schedule them both for the same shift at least once a week.

"Isn't tonight the open mic night?" Alex asked.

"It's my first one. I hope people come," Anna said.

"It sounds like fun, and you have the perfect weather for it," Velma said. "Richie and I are having dinner with some friends at the *Sand Dollar Grille*, but I'm hoping we'll finish in time to stop by."

"I'll try to come back tonight too. I have plans with some friends, but I'll try to break away. What time is it at?" Alex asked.

"7:00," Anna said.

When Jack heard that Alex was planning to return, he announced that he would try to come back, too.

"I'll do my best, as well," Emily, another college student, said.

"You guys are the best," Anna said. "The more people present the better."

While they were talking, Anna's cell phone rang. She saw that it was Ellen, so she took the call in her office.

"Hi, Ellen."

"Hi, Anna. I know it's late notice, but Wil, Luke's friend from high school, is coming over for coffee this afternoon. He'll be here at 2:00, and I'm planning to ask him what happened between him and Luke. Are you able to break away from work?"

"I think I can manage that. Text me your address and I'll do my best."

Shortly before 2:00, it was clear that Velma, Alex, Emily,

and Jack had things under control at *Bella's Dream*, so Anna slipped out to go to Ellen's.

A few minutes later, she pulled up to a white Cape Cod-style home with black shutters and an attached two-car garage.

Ellen answered the door and greeted Anna. "Olivia is going out with a friend after school, and Caleb went into the office for the afternoon, so it will be just us and Wil. It will be easier for us to ask Wil some questions without the others around."

Anna helped Ellen put out a coffeecake and condiments for coffee, and before they had finished, the doorbell rang. It was Wil. He handed Ellen a white paper bag. "I brought some muffins and Danishes."

"How thoughtful," Ellen said, accepting the bag.

Wil hugged Ellen. "I'm so very sorry about Luke. I know how much you loved him."

"I loved my baby brother so much," Ellen said. "I was twelve when he was born, and I used to pretend he was my baby."

Wil squeezed Ellen's hand. "He loved you very much, too."

When they came into the dining room, Wil was surprised to see Anna.

"This is my friend, Anna McBride. She stopped by to offer her condolences, so I invited her to stay for a little while."

"Nice to meet you, Anna."

"Why don't we have a seat? I just brewed a fresh pot of coffee."

The three of them sat at the farmhouse table, which ran parallel to a bay window. Anna could easily imagine Olivia and her family having Sunday dinners and holidays around that table. She thought back to her own childhood when her parents, siblings, aunts, uncles, and cousins gathered every Sunday after Mass to share a meal together. Where had the time gone?

Ellen put the muffins and Danishes that Wil had brought on a yellow serving dish, sliced the coffeecake, and poured them each a cup. Then they each chose a baked good.

"How is everyone doing?" Wil asked Ellen. "I can't imagine what you and your family must be going through."

"It feels like a nightmare that we can't wake up from. I keep expecting Luke to walk through my door or call at any moment."

"I know what you mean," Wil said. "How is the investigation going? Are the police close to figuring out who did this?"

"Charlie is giving this case his full attention, so I'm sure it's only a matter of time." Ellen paused, as if searching for the right words. "I just wanted you to know that I spoke with Nina after Luke's death, and she said how much Luke regretted stealing from you a couple of years ago."

Wil's eyes flew open. "I didn't even know you were aware of that."

"Luke told me," Ellen said. "It was one of his biggest regrets."

"I'm not going to lie. It took a long time for me to forgive him, but I'm glad I did."

"Wil, if you don't mind my asking, I told Luke to invite you to Sunday dinner a couple of weeks before he died, but he said that the two of you had a falling out. Can I ask what happened?"

Wil looked as if Ellen had slapped him.

"Of course, if you'd rather not talk about it, I understand," she quickly added.

Will started to speak, but then stopped himself. "If you don't mind, I think it's best that I don't."

Anna studied Wil while he and Ellen talked.

"I understand," Ellen said, backing off.

"It's hard to imagine that someone would have wanted to hurt Luke, especially now that he was getting his life in order," Anna said, trying to lead the conversation without directly asking Wil about Luke's potential enemies. After all, Wil and Anna had just met, so it might be an awkward question coming from her.

"I had the same thought," Wil said. "It doesn't make sense."

Fortunately, Ellen followed Anna's lead.

"Wil, you were my brother's oldest friend. Can you think of anyone who would do this?"

"I've been wondering that same thing ever since Monday, and I can't think of anyone who would have wanted to kill Luke. If I had to guess, I'd say that it was likely someone from when he was..." Wil hesitated, apparently searching for the best words. "From when he went through that rough patch."

"I know you weren't in his life at that time, but is there anyone who comes to mind?" Ellen asked.

"When Luke came to my house that time - when he stole the money from me - there was another guy with them. He was waiting in the car with Nina, but I could see him through my living room window. I asked who he was, and Luke said that he was Nina's brother, Chris. I had almost forgotten about him until I saw him talking to Luke in the middle of Main Street."

"When was this?" Anna asked, aghast.

"About a month ago. I went into *Cove Coffee* to grab a coffee to go, and Luke and Charlie were having breakfast. I didn't want to interrupt their conversation, so I just waved. They must have been finishing breakfast, because Charlie left while I was ordering, and Luke went to the restroom. As I was leaving, I got a phone call, so I sat in my car to take the call. That's when I saw Chris approach Luke. I couldn't hear anything, but he appeared to be yelling at Luke. Chris angrily stormed off after a couple of minutes."

Anna and Ellen looked at one another.

"Nina didn't mention that Chris was there the night Luke asked you for money," Anna said.

"Have you told the police about Chris?" Ellen asked.

Wil shook his head. "I just remembered. When I talked to Charlie Doyle, I was so shaken up by what happened to Luke, that it didn't occur to me. But I'll be sure to tell him."

"Thank you," Ellen said. "And please give my best to Danielle. I was so happy to hear that the two of you got back together."

A broad smile swept across Wil's face. "I definitely will."

CHAPTER 11

Ellen walked Wil to the door, then returned to the dining room table, where Anna was still sitting. "Wil clearly didn't want to talk about whatever happened between him and Luke."

"*That* was obvious," Anna said, taking another muffin. "He admitted that something else had happened between them recently. The question is, was it something that could be a motive for murder, or was it just a spat between friends?"

Ellen leaned back in her honey-colored chair. "I really wish we knew what happened."

"Is there anyone else who could shed more light on the situation?" Anna asked. "Perhaps Luke and Wil had a mutual friend who might know what happened between them."

"There's nobody who immediately comes to mind, but I'll give it some thought."

"In the meantime, we need to talk to this Chris guy," Anna said.

"That was the first I'd ever heard of Nina having a brother.

Luke never mentioned him before, so I doubt that they remained friends."

"If that's the case, we need to know why Chris was in Seagull Cove talking to Luke shortly before Luke was murdered. I think that a conversation with Chris should be our top priority."

"Agreed," Ellen said. "The wake is tomorrow, so I doubt I'll be able to focus on the investigation for the next couple of days. How about if we visit Loni today and get it over with, since that should be the easiest conversation?" Ellen suggested. "Then we can talk to Chris after the funeral is over. I know where Loni's office is. We could just pop by."

"Let's do it."

They took two cars to Loni's office on Main Street and parked in front of a wooden structure with a sign on the front that read, "Devereaux Insurance Agency." The door was unlocked, so they walked in.

"I was hoping we could speak with Loni Devereaux," Ellen said to the receptionist.

"Do you have an appointment?" the young woman asked.

"No, but if you tell her that Luke Carter's sister is here, I think she'll speak with us," Anna said.

The young woman disappeared into a hallway leading to the back of the building and returned a couple of minutes later with another woman who appeared to be in her early fifties. She had straight brown hair and was wearing grey slacks and a cranberry and cream-colored sleeveless V-neck blouse.

Ellen extended her hand. "My name is Ellen Montgomery. I understand you knew my brother, Luke Carter."

"Loni Devereaux," the woman said as she stiffly shook Ellen's hand. "I'm sorry for your loss."

"Thank you."

"I met Luke once or twice, but I wouldn't say that I *knew* him," Loni said.

"I was hoping you could spare a few minutes, anyway. We had some questions that you might be able to answer."

"My next client will be in shortly, but I suppose I could spare a few minutes. Although, I don't know how I could possibly help you."

"It won't take long," Anna said.

Loni led the women to a stylish office and closed the door.

"We'll get right to the point," Anna said. "We understand that you and Luke were fierce competitors."

Loni shrugged her shoulders matter-of-factly. "It's a fiercely competitive industry."

"Fair enough," Ellen said. "I don't know much about Luke's colleagues, but he obviously had at least one enemy. I was hoping you could tell me if you knew of anyone who had it out for my brother."

Loni studied them. "As I said, it's a very competitive industry, but I've never heard of someone killing another insurance agent over a client. I know every agent in the area, and as far as I know, nobody is unstable. Or at least *that* unstable."

"I suppose that makes sense," Ellen said. "But the fact remains, my brother didn't have any enemies, yet someone killed him. I suppose I'm grasping at straws, but I was hoping you might know something that I don't."

Loni reflected. "Let me put it this way. I don't know of any agents who would resort to something like that just to eliminate the competition. Although..." Loni paused. "Luke did have one rather odd client that I know of."

"Philip Pearson," Anna supplied.

Loni nodded. "I'm not going to lie. Luke and I competed for Philip's business, and I was disappointed when Philip went with Luke instead. After the incident with his house, I reached out to him again, and he is now with me. But I wish I hadn't. The guy is very high-maintenance. He's not worth the commission I earn from his policy. If I were the police, he would be my top suspect."

"I tend to agree," Ellen said. "Philip is on our radar. Is there anyone else you can think of?"

There was a knock on the door.

"Come in, Tina," Loni said.

The receptionist poked her head in the door. "Your next appointment is here."

Loni stood up. "I'm afraid I can't keep this client waiting. There isn't anyone else I can think of. Again, I'm sorry for your loss."

Loni ushered Anna and Ellen out the door before they could even thank her for her time. Or ask her if she had an alibi.

On their way out, Anna pointed to the business hours, which were printed on Loni's door. "Her office doesn't open until 9:00 and she wasn't wearing a wedding ring, so she likely doesn't have an alibi."

"Do you think she could have done it?" Ellen asked, as she walked Anna to her car.

"She's not the *warmest* person in the world, but her motive is weak. And she *did* bring up a good point. It's a competitive industry, and she's been in it for a long time. If she went around killing all her competitors, she'd be in jail by now. We can keep her on our list of suspects, but as far as I'm concerned, she's at the bottom of that list."

"Agreed," Ellen said.

"I'd better get to work. Please give Olivia my best. I'll be thinking of you both and keeping you in prayer over the next few days."

Anna was about to get into her car when she remembered something. "I almost forgot. We're having an open mic night tonight at *Bella's Dream*. If you and your family are looking to get out of the house, it should be fun."

"I don't think I'm in the mood for something like that quite yet, but thank you."

"I understand."

When Anna returned to *Bella's Dream*, Joe Wiggins had just arrived for his daily scoop. Anna was glad that she had taken her own car to Ellen's. If Joe had seen her getting out of Ellen's car yet again, he would have peppered her with questions.

"Velma tells me you're having your first open mic night tonight," Joe said.

"I'm a little nervous about it," Anna said, as she tied on her apron. "I hope people come. I hung fliers all over Main Street, and I've been posting about it all over our social media sites."

While Joe was savoring his ice cream, Anna sat on the stool next to him.

Joe chuckled. "Usually when you sit here, you have something important you want to talk about."

Anna had to laugh at Joe's perceptiveness. "You're right."

"Is it about your sister?"

"Right again, Joe."

"Ah, I figured that you wouldn't let too much time go by before taking action after our conversation with Jeremy. Did you go through Bella's paperwork?"

"I spent a couple of hours last night combing through Bella's personal financial records, and I discovered a few really interesting things."

Joe finished his last spoonful of ice cream and threw his napkin inside the dish. Velma cleared it away and refilled his water.

"What did you discover?" Joe asked.

"First, Bella had a retirement account with about $75,000 in it. Shortly before the accident, she told me that she was going to close out the account and use the money to pay off some debt. I didn't think too much of it. The first couple of years of our practice, we both had to tighten our belts. We didn't earn much money, and we each invested our savings into the business. I figured that she must have accumulated some credit card debt and wanted to pay it off."

"Makes sense," Joe said. "But $75,000 is a heck of a lot of credit card debt."

"Exactly," Anna said. "Since I knew that she had closed out the account, I didn't look at the statements after she died. I was more interested in closing her current accounts and notifying her creditors of her death. I didn't see any reason to go digging through her retirement account back then. I never realized she had had *that* much money in her 401k, or I would have questioned where it went."

"I see your point."

"That's not all. Last night, I scrutinized her credit card accounts, and, Joe, she never had *any* significant debt. With very little exception, she paid off her credit card bill at the end of every month. I went back seven years. During our first year in business, she carried a balance for six months. However, she paid that off years ago. At the time she closed out her retirement account, she had literally no debt. Again, I never thought to look through her old credit card statements to see how much debt she carried. I had no reason to question anything that she told me, and it wasn't any of my business, anyway."

Anna closed her eyes as the pain of those days rushed back. "All I wanted to do in those early days was to get that paperwork over with so I could focus on dealing with the loss of my sister. But now that I know she withdrew $75,000 and didn't have any debt, I have to know where that money went. Of course, she would have paid penalties for early withdrawal, but still, that's a good chunk of change. And there was also a savings account that she emptied shortly before her death, which amounted to another $10,000."

"Let me guess. You're thinking that Bella staged her death and used the money to start over in another state."

"That's a definite possibility. Where else would the money be, if not with my sister?"

"She could have had some debt that you didn't know about," Joe suggested.

"I suppose that's possible, but as far as I know, I have all of her financial records. I have seven years' worth of statements for all of her accounts. It's possible that she owed a friend some money that I didn't know about, but I find that unlikely. Especially not *that* much money."

"Did she make any major purchases shortly before her death? Perhaps a car? Or did she pay down a mortgage?"

"Nothing. She rented her apartment, and she would never

have withdrawn money from her retirement account to buy a car. We had the same accountant, and I can guarantee you that he would have advised against that."

Joe furrowed his brow. "That *is* strange."

"I'm not sure what to do next," Anna said. "I suppose I could talk to some of her friends to see if she confided in any of them, but I don't want to upset them. If I start asking questions about her behavior before her death, they are going to want to know why, and I don't want to give them false hope. The person who knew her the best besides me was her boyfriend, Grayson. But I'm afraid I would either upset Grayson, or he would be worried about me for bringing up the possibility that my sister staged her own death. If he knew what I was thinking, he might tell Albie."

"Sounds like you have some strategizing to do. And I agree, I think I'd want to have something a little more solid before upsetting peoples' lives. As compelling as it is, all of the evidence you have is still circumstantial."

Anna knew that, strictly speaking, Joe was right. But at the same time, she also knew how close she and Bella had been. They were transparent with one another about everything, including their finances. Especially after they opened the practice together. There was nothing that Bella could have needed all that money for. And besides, even if Anna's theory was wrong, where did all that money go?

"Cheer up, kiddo. You'll figure out what to do next. The answer will come to you when you least expect it."

"Thanks for being such a good sounding board, Joe. If it weren't for you, I wouldn't have anyone to talk to about this. Your perspective and experience are invaluable."

Joe looked at Anna with compassion. "I know this is hard.

And I can't say I blame you for wanting to get to the bottom of what happened. But I also don't want to see you end up disappointed. If you find out that Bella did, indeed, die in that boating accident, it will be like losing her all over again. It very well may not have been Bella who I saw peering into your shop from across the street the day of your grand opening. I didn't see her up close, so it's possible it was just someone who looked like her. And as for what you discovered last night, in my years as a private investigator, the one thing I've learned over and over again is that people often have secrets. It doesn't mean it's sinister. People hold back more from their loved ones than you'd think. Maybe she had some financial concerns that she didn't want to burden you with."

It *would* be like Bella not to want to burden her loved ones with her own problems.

"I understand that, Joe. And I know that I could be setting myself up to get hurt. That's exactly why I'm not telling anybody else who loved Bella what I am doing. But you have to understand that I couldn't live with myself if I didn't seek answers to these questions. The wondering would be worse than any disappointment I might experience. We're talking about my little sister."

"I understand where you're coming from," Joe said. "I don't envy your position."

When Anna and Joe had begun talking, Velma was within earshot. However, as soon as Bella's name came up, she found some busywork for herself and the other employees to do in between customers, so they wouldn't overhear their conversation.

After Joe left, Velma handed Anna a mint chocolate chip

ice cream cone, one of Anna's favorite flavors. "Here. You look like you could use this," she said with a warm smile.

"Thanks," Anna said, gratefully accepting the cone.

When Anna finished her ice cream, Velma helped her set up the microphone for the open mic night.

CHAPTER 12

At 6:30, business started to pick up, and Anna was hopeful that they would have a decent turn out for the open mic night.

Anna was crossing her fingers that Ruthie would be the first to take the microphone. She arrived at *Bella's Dream* a few minutes before 7:00, looking as if she might hightail it out of there at any moment.

Anna went straight over to Ruthie and put her arm around her shoulders for moral support. Ruthie glanced around at the crowd that had gathered in the dining room. "I can't believe I let you talk me into this, Anna McBride. I never share my poetry with anyone, and now I'm about to do a reading for anyone in Seagull Cove who happens to show up. I haven't eaten a thing all day."

"I'll give you all the ice cream you can eat on the house after your reading," Anna promised. "You have nothing to worry about. Your poem is amazing. I wouldn't have suggested that you read it tonight if I thought you'd make a fool of yourself."

Anna could see the doubt, which remained in Ruthie's eyes.

Velma, Richie, and a couple of their friends walked in while Anna was attempting to calm Ruthie down, so Anna left her in Velma's and Richie's capable and encouraging hands while she greeted some of her other customers. Many of her employees who weren't scheduled to work that night made an appearance, including Alex and Jack. They were all sharing a couple of tables they had pulled together at the back of the dining room.

At 7:00, Anna took the microphone. "I am thrilled to welcome you to the first-ever open mic night at *Bella's Dream*. I hope tonight will be the first of many such events, and that you will all come to think of this little ice cream shop as a second home."

The crowd responded with applause.

"Our first performance tonight will be a poetry reading from Seagull Cove's own Ruthie Valentino. I'm sure you all know her from her wonderful bookstore, *The Book Cove*."

Ruthie was greeted with another warm round of applause as she took the stage. Her first few words were tentative and shaky, but after the first stanza, she seemed to realize that everyone was listening intently to her words, and she gained confidence. She finished her poem about a cottage by the sea to a standing ovation.

By the time Ruthie stepped away from the microphone and joined Anna, who had been watching from the back of the dining room, she was smiling from ear to ear.

"They *loved* you, Ruthie!" Anna exclaimed, as Ruthie received several pats on the back from people she knew.

After Ruthie, a young woman bravely stepped up to sing a

song she had written. She was followed by several others. With a constant line of customers at the register throughout the entire evening, Anna was glad she had scheduled an extra employee so that she was able to mingle and enjoy the night. By the end of the evening, Anna didn't know if she or Ruthie was more thrilled at how successful the event had gone.

At 9:00, the last performer finished. Several attendees had encouraged Ruthie to publish a collection of her poems and to sell it in her bookstore.

"It looks like Seagull Cove will soon be able to boast a published poet," Velma said when she came over to congratulate Ruthie. "And to think it all started right here in *Bella's Dream*. My friends and I loved your poem. You can count on us to purchase a copy when you publish your first collection."

"We'll expect a *signed* copy," Richie added.

Anna couldn't have been happier to hear them say that.

"Absolutely," Ruthie said. "And thank you for being so encouraging. I have never been so scared in my whole life. It's one thing to talk to customers about other people's work, but reading my own was a giant leap out of my comfort zone."

"You did great," Anna said. "The next time it will be much easier."

Anna got two scoops of rum raisin, Ruthie's favorite ice cream flavor, and handed it to her. "You earned this."

Ruthie accepted it with a grateful smile. "I did."

"There were so many musicians tonight that I was thinking we should try a karaoke night," Velma said. "I think it would be a huge draw."

"Great idea. Let's get it in the books," Anna said.

It was wonderful to have something positive to focus on amidst all of the investigating Anna found herself involved in.

She felt like she was walking on air until Casper arrived for his nightly meal. The little guy still appeared melancholy, which reminded Anna that Luke's killer was still out there somewhere.

As if reading her thoughts, while Anna was cleaning Casper's bowl, Ellen knocked on the glass door.

"Hi, Anna. Do you have a moment?"

"Of course. Come on in," Anna said.

They sat at one of the round marble bistro tables overlooking Main Street. There were still a few people milling about, probably on their way home after a late dinner or a drink with friends.

"Olivia and I considered coming to your open mic night tonight, but we weren't in the mood to be around so many people quite yet."

"That's completely understandable," Anna said. "Don't worry, there will be plenty more in the future. It was a smashing success."

"That's great. Olivia will be pleased to hear that. She wanted me to let you know that she'll be available to start working again next week. I think it will be good for her to get back into a normal routine."

"You're probably right. I'll put her back on the schedule starting Monday."

"Thank you. That's not why I came by, though. I was hoping to catch you before you left for the night. I was at Luke's rental apartment this afternoon cleaning out his possessions, and I ran into his landlord, Rob, who lives upstairs from Luke. I asked him if he noticed anything unusual in the days leading up to Luke's death, and he told me that someone came to visit Luke a few days before his death.

There was a lot of yelling, so Rob came downstairs to see what was going on. He thinks the visitor was high because of the way he was acting. Luke was calmly asking the man to leave, but he refused. He said that he needed to settle something with Luke first. When Rob threatened to call the police, the man finally left. On a hunch, I called up a social media picture of Nina's brother, Chris, on my phone. He was easy to find because there were some photos with him and Nina that she had tagged. Anyway, I figured that if he had caused trouble with Luke after his breakfast with Charlie, as Wil said, perhaps he returned to pick up the conversation where he left off. Rob confirmed that it was, in fact, Chris who was yelling at Luke that night."

"Did he say what they were arguing about?" Anna asked.

"He didn't hear what was being said. He only knew that Chris was pretty upset about something."

"Now more than ever we *definitely* need to talk to Nina again," Anna said. "She's the only one I can think of who might know what their conversations were about."

"My thoughts exactly. But I don't think we should talk to her alone this time, just in case Chris is there."

"Or in case she and Chris are working together," Anna added.

"I hadn't thought of that. I'll ask Caleb to come with us. He's not going to like that we're poking around, but I know he'd like it even worse if we went alone. I'll be back in touch after the services are over."

"Sounds like a plan," Anna said.

After Ellen left, Anna locked up the shop and returned home. Between thoughts of the successful open mic night, the investigation into Luke's murder, and what she had discovered about Bella's finances swirling around in her mind, Anna couldn't sleep. So, she made herself some mint tea and watched a movie before turning in.

As soon as the shop opened on Friday morning, Charlie came into the store. He looked like a man on a mission.

"Hi, Charlie," Velma said. "It's nice to see you here. What can I get for you?"

"I'm actually not here for the ice cream. Anna, we need to talk about Luke Carson's case."

"Of course," Anna said, leading him to a booth in the dining room.

"I told you everything that I saw on Monday morning, so I don't think I have any more information to add to my statement. But I'll do my best to answer your questions."

"I don't have any more questions, exactly," Charlie said. His mouth was moving but the rest of his face was stiff. "It's more like a request."

"I don't understand," Anna said. Although that wasn't entirely true. She had a feeling she knew what this was about.

"I just had a conversation with Philip Pearson. I understand that you and Ellen paid him a visit and were asking some questions."

They were busted. There was nothing Anna could do now but to come clean. "That's true. Ellen asked me if I would help her try to figure out what happened to her brother."

"And since you have a sister who was tragically taken from you, you didn't feel you could say no, right?"

Anna was glad he at least understood that she wasn't just being a busy-body. "That pretty much sums it up. Ellen heard that Joe and I helped find Marcus Grady's killer last month, and she asked for my help. I tried to say no, but I couldn't refuse her request in the end."

"Look, Anna, I understand your feelings. Really, I do. But this is not something you should be getting involved in. I am following up on every lead, including Philip. If you keep at this, you're either going to get yourself hurt or impede our investigation. I need you to stay out of it. I know that your intentions are good, but don't forget what happened last time. You and Joe were almost killed." Charlie looked directly into her eyes and held her gaze for a moment. "I don't think your family could handle losing another child."

Ouch. That hurt. Anna hadn't thought of it from that perspective.

"I also had a talk with Ellen earlier this morning, and I think I managed to convince her to back off. I don't think she will be asking for any more help in finding Luke's killer."

Anna was somewhat relieved to hear that Charlie had already talked to Ellen. He was probably right. Eventually, the police would find the killer. They just needed to be patient. At least now she could focus on her own sister's case.

"Okay, then," Anna said. "It's settled." Besides, Ellen would need all of her energy to get through the next couple of days since the funeral services were taking place today and tomorrow.

Charlie gave Anna a relieved smile. "I'm glad to hear that we agree on this, Anna."

"Of course. Despite what you think, I don't go looking to get involved in murder investigations. I just couldn't say no to a grieving sister. But I'm happy to stay out of it."

"In that case, I won't breathe a word of this to Joe Wiggins.

I was considering having him keep an eye on you, but it doesn't look like there's any need for that, after all."

"Definitely not," Anna said. Joe's concern for her was touching, but she didn't need him questioning her every move.

They both stood up from the booth, and Charlie smiled playfully. "You know, I think I have time for a quick ice cream cone before I leave."

CHAPTER 13

Friday was another busy day at *Bella's Dream*. There was a lot of buzz about the open mic night the previous evening, and there were several requests for Anna to hold another one. She happily promised her customers that she would schedule one for the following month and that if interest remained, it could potentially become a monthly event.

Anna also informally polled her customers to gauge interest in a karaoke night, and most seemed enthusiastic about the idea. It looked like *Bella's Dream* was well on its way to being the community hub that Anna had hoped it would become. Her sister's dream was becoming a reality, and Anna was enjoying the journey more than she imagined.

When Velma's shift ended at 5:00, Anna and Velma decided to visit the funeral home where Luke's wake was being held to pay their respects. They each went home to change into more appropriate clothes, and Anna picked Velma up at her house at 6:00.

Much of the town had shown up to Luke's funeral, and the receiving line stretched all the way to the door.

As they took their place in the line, Anna noticed Nina, who was about twenty people ahead of them in the line. She hoped that Nina's presence didn't make it more difficult for Ellen, given what they had recently learned about Chris. It took all Anna's strength to resist the temptation to ask Nina about her brother, but she didn't want to break her promise to Charlie. Besides, it wasn't the time or the place.

And it was a good thing she resisted. A couple of minutes later, Charlie walked in with his wife, Patty.

Patty immediately came over to greet Anna. The two women had become acquainted in the weeks following Bella's death, and Anna had always like Patty. "It's so good to see you. I just wish it wasn't under these horrible circumstances."

Anna nodded. "It's good to see you, too."

"Every time I've walked by your ice cream parlor, it's been busy inside. It looks like business is going well."

Velma told Patty about the open mic night, Ruthie's poetry reading, and their plans to make it a monthly event. "We're also going to try running a karaoke evening. You should join our newsletter list so that you can stay up to date and check out some of the events. It would be a fun night out with some friends or with Charlie if you can get a babysitter."

Patty gave Anna her email address.

When they finally made their way to the front of the line, a weary Ellen and Olivia seemed happy to see the four of them.

"We are doing everything we possibly can to bring Luke's killer to justice," Charlie assured Ellen.

"I know you are. And thank you for coming tonight. Luke

had a lot of respect and admiration for you. Thank you for being his friend and mentor when he needed one the most."

Anna and Velma hugged Ellen and Olivia.

"If there is anything we can do for you, please don't hesitate to ask," Anna said. "Take as long as you need before returning to work. Your mom told me to put you back on next week's schedule, but if you change your mind, we can find someone to cover your shifts."

"I still want to come back next week. I'm ready for things to return to normal. Or at least as normal as they can for now. Besides, I miss everyone."

"We miss you, too," Velma said.

Charlie had to return to work since he was busy with the case, and Patty didn't want to leave their kids alone for very long. Their oldest was at a friend's house, and she was afraid the younger three might get into trouble if she left them for too long. So, the couple left as soon as they paid their respects to the family and said a prayer by Luke's casket.

Anna and Velma stepped into the adjoining room for a few minutes to admire the photos of Luke that the family had set up on poster boards as a tribute.

Velma needed to go to the ladies' room before they left, so Anna sat down and waited. She was surprised to see Ellen approach her. Ellen led her to a corner, where they could speak in private.

"I have to get back to the line in a minute, but I was hoping to catch you alone before you left. Did Charlie talk to you?"

"Yes. He made me promise not to investigate anymore. He said that you were on board with the idea."

"I am. Charlie talked some sense into me. I'm sorry I allowed you to put yourself in danger. I don't know what I was thinking. Charlie is right. We should leave the investigating to the police."

"Given the situation, it's probably for the best. Although, I have to admit, I was tempted to talk to Nina tonight to ask her what her brother was doing at Luke's apartment and what he was arguing with him about on Main Street shortly before Luke's death."

"Me, too," Ellen said. "It was so hard to bite my tongue and not say anything when she came through the line. But even if we were still investigating, she has a right to mourn like everyone else. As long as she's not the killer, that is. She and my brother were close at one point. I told Charlie about what Luke's landlord said, so he's going to look into it." Ellen glanced back at the line. "I'd better get back. Thanks for coming. It means a lot to Olivia and me."

"Of course. When this is all over, let's have lunch."

"Or ice cream," Ellen said.

"Anytime. You know where to find me."

Velma returned just after Ellen left. On their way out of the funeral home, Anna spotted several of her employees waiting to express their condolences. She wasn't surprised to see Jack, since he and Olivia were in the same class and had known each other before working together at *Bella's Dream*. But as far as Anna knew, the others didn't know Olivia outside of work. It warmed her heart to see that her employees had formed a bond working together at her shop. *Bella's Dream* really was becoming a little community.

After dropping Velma off at home, Anna returned to work. However, since her employees had things under control, there was no reason she couldn't take the rest of the evening off.

Anna stopped at the bakery for some fresh bread before

walking home. Then she picked a tomato that had ripened early from her little garden, a generous handful of fresh basil from one of the potted plants on her front porch, and added some fresh mozzarella cheese, which she had in her fridge. Then she put a generous handful of Cape Cod potato chips onto her plate and brought her dinner to the table on the front porch to enjoy the summer evening.

The scent of herbs mingled with the smell of flowers as she enjoyed her meal. She thought of her successful open mic night the previous day and how Bella's dream was growing into a reality. Even amidst all the uncertainty she was feeling, a wave of joy swept over her.

Anna glanced at the chair across the table. The only thing that would make this moment even more perfect was if Bella were there to share it with her.

Her thoughts drifted to Bella's financial paperwork. Now that she was stepping away from Luke's investigation, she would have more time to plot her next move.

When she finished her sandwich, Anna leaned back in her chair. Was she just fooling herself? Could there be a logical explanation for why Bella withdrew the funds from her retirement account? Maybe she really *had* carried credit card debt, and for whatever reason, the statements from that credit card were not with the rest of her paperwork. Bella could have closed out the account after she paid the balance and threw away the statements. But still, while Bella did have an impulsive streak, it went against her character to accumulate $75,000 worth of credit card debt. And that didn't even include the $10,000 that she withdrew from her savings account. Anna needed to follow these leads to their end, or she'd be wondering about it for the rest of her life.

Anna revisited the idea of talking to Grayson to see if he knew anything about it. However, as much as she wanted to confide in Grayson, she just couldn't bring herself to do anything that might raise his hopes. She couldn't do that to him after so many years. She would have to think of another idea.

CHAPTER 14

On Saturday morning, Anna woke up before her alarm went off. Since she still had a few hours before she needed to be at work, she pulled some weeds from her garden, changed into her bathing suit and beach coverup, and headed to the cove for a morning swim.

The crowds hadn't yet arrived, so she largely had the beach to herself, with the exception of a few fishermen and early morning walkers.

When she got tired of swimming, Anna dried off and stretched out on her oversized beach towel for the next hour, allowing the sunshine to warm her skin.

Feeling refreshed and rejuvenated, Anna walked back to her cottage and showered off the salt water and sand. Then she had a leisurely breakfast in her living room and made her way to *Bella's Dream*.

The foot traffic was nonstop from the time Anna opened her doors straight through until closing time. Anna spent most of the day providing backup for her employees behind the counter, in order to keep the lines moving along smoothly.

When she wasn't needed behind the counter, she greeted her guests and chatted up tourists.

The day flew by, and before Anna knew it, the evening shift was over. She took the trash to the dumpster while her employees cleaned the store. When she was heading back inside, she was startled to see Casper sitting on the stoop.

"Where did *you* come from?" she asked him with a chuckle.

He thumped his tail against the concrete and glared at her with his green eyes.

"Oh, I see. You're mad at me, because I wasn't here last night to feed you. I promise to remind my employees not to forget about you in the future." She scratched the top of his head and since he didn't pull away, Anna took that as a sign that she was forgiven. She filled his bowl with tuna and remained on the back stoop while he ate.

When she returned inside, Anna was surprised to see Ellen sitting at one of the bistro tables. Anna went over and took the seat across from her.

"I'm surprised to see you here. Wasn't Luke's funeral this morning?"

Ellen nodded. "Yes. Then the family went back to my house for a reception afterward. I came by because there's something I need to tell you."

"We're just about to close. If you can hang on for a few minutes, we can have some privacy."

As soon as the strawberry ice cream cone clock on the wall next to the counter struck 10:00, Anna flipped the sign on her door to read "closed," her employees left, and she joined Ellen at the marble bistro table.

"What is so important that you came here on the night of Luke's funeral?" Anna asked.

Ellen took a deep breath. "I have had quite the day. After everyone left my house, I was feeling restless. I wanted to be alone, but I also felt like I needed to keep busy to get my mind off of everything. So, I went over to Luke's apartment to do some more cleaning. There are still a couple of weeks before the end of July, when I need to have everything cleared out, but the sooner I can put that task behind me, the better. Luke's apartment is on the ground level of a double decker, and when I pulled into the driveway behind his landlord's car, I thought I saw someone climbing out the living room window and running through the bushes. But then I convinced myself that I must have just scared away a cat or some other animal. Anyway, when I went inside, I saw that someone had clearly been in there."

"What do you mean? Was something missing?"

"I don't think so, but there were footprints on the vinyl floor from a man's shoes. Whoever was there left in a hurry and didn't have time to clean up after himself."

"Are you sure it wasn't from the police? One of the crime scene technicians could have left it."

"I'm positive. They finished searching Luke's apartment a couple of days after his death and told me that they wouldn't be going back. I've been in there since then, and those footprints weren't in there. I think whoever it was probably figured I wouldn't be at Luke's today because it was the day of his funeral."

"You could be right," Anna said.

"I went upstairs to see if Rob was home, but he didn't hear anything. He called the police and Charlie came right over. It was such an emotional day, and I couldn't take anymore drama, so I left as soon as I told him what happened. He's still at Luke's. I know we're not investigating anymore, but I thought I'd update you, anyway. I didn't feel like going straight home, so I came here first."

"I'm glad you came, Ellen. I'm so sorry you had to go through that on the day of your brother's funeral, especially when all you wanted to do was clean out his apartment in peace."

"Thanks, Anna. I always feel better after talking to you. By the way, Olivia is looking forward to coming back to work on Monday."

"I'm looking forward to having her back. We've all missed her this week."

Ellen smiled. "Well, I should get going. I'll keep you posted."

Just as Ellen was about to leave, her cell phone rang. She looked at the screen. "It's Charlie." She accepted the call. "Hi, Charlie. Oh, my goodness, are you absolutely *sure* it was him? I see. Well thank you for letting me know. Please keep me updated."

Ellen disconnected the call and stared blankly out the window.

"What did he say?" Anna asked.

"Apparently, a lot happened after I left. The police are holding Chris for questioning."

"So, it *was* Chris who broke into Luke's apartment?"

"It appears that way. Charlie found him on foot not too far from Luke's apartment. He lives a few towns away, so Charlie thought it was odd that he'd be in Seagull Cove on the same night that Luke's apartment was broken into. Charlie examined the bottom of Chris's shoe, and the size and pattern was an exact match to the footprint that was left at Luke's apartment. The police are questioning Chris and are planning to hold him overnight."

"That's great news," Anna said. "It sounds like the police may have solved the case."

"It's quite possible. Why else would Chris have broken into Luke's apartment if it weren't to remove evidence of some sort?" Ellen asked.

"Although, you *did* say that the police searched Luke's apartment immediately following his death," Anna said.

"Yes. They were in there all day Monday."

"I wonder why Chris would be going to Luke's apartment *now*?" Anna asked. "If he's the killer and there was any evidence pointing to him, he must know that the police would already have found it. Why would he break in today?"

"I don't know," Ellen said. "Maybe he's not that bright. But Chris's footprint matched the one I saw at Luke's, and Charlie has him for questioning. So, there *must* be a reason."

Something didn't sit right with Anna. But who knew, maybe Chris believed that the police missed something, and tonight was his chance, since the family would be occupied with the funeral? "Hopefully, Charlie is figuring it all out as we speak."

CHAPTER 15

On Sunday morning, while Anna was watering her English garden, Ellen called.

"I just talked to Charlie. The police are still holding Chris, but they are going to have to let him go today. Charlie doesn't have enough evidence to charge him for anything."

"Did he admit to being in Luke's apartment?"

"According to Charlie, Chris won't talk. At all. He demanded a lawyer, and the lawyer is insisting that the police let him go. They don't have enough evidence to charge him for either breaking and entering or murder. Chris *did* admit to being in Luke's apartment the week before Luke's death. He claims that the footprint must be from then. But, Anna, there was no footprint in Luke's foyer the last time I was there, which was immediately after his death."

"I'm sure the crime scene technicians took photos of Luke's apartment," Anna said.

"That's true. I didn't think of that. I just don't know how much more of this I can take."

"Between two visits to Luke's apartment and the scene he

made on Main Street after Luke's breakfast with Charlie, he's hiding something. If Chris is the killer, I'm sure it's only a matter of time until Charlie arrests him."

"I hope you're right."

"Thanks for the update. Keep me posted. I'm heading to Mass. I'll say a prayer that Luke's killer is caught soon."

"I'll be in touch if I receive any more information," Ellen said. "And thank you."

After Mass, Anna came home and changed, then walked to work, ready for another busy day. By the time she opened the shop, the downtown streets were already bustling with activity. They had their usual after-lunch rush, so Anna stuck around to back up her employees. Although, she didn't have to. With all of the customers who had been coming through the doors of *Bella's Dream*, everyone was getting plenty of practice and had their jobs down pat.

Anna was going to miss her college student employees when they headed back to school in late August. She had become accustomed to seeing their faces every day.

Just after the rush died down, Todd Devonshire came into Anna's shop. Todd was a charming financial advisor who stopped in from time to time, when he had an appointment with a client in Seagull Cove. Velma had initially pointed out the fact that he was single, but Anna had no desire to complicate her life right now with a relationship.

"Hi, Todd. Don't tell me that you're meeting with a client on a Sunday," Anna said.

He flashed her his usual charming smile. "Can't I just come to Seagull Cove for a cold treat at my favorite ice cream shop?"

"Of course you can, but it seems like a long drive for an ice cream when there are plenty of shops closer to home." Todd lived in Marblehead, which was a few towns away.

"Okay, you caught me. I'm meeting some friends at the Beach in a little while, and I got to town early. It looks like business is strong."

"Business has been great," Anna said. "I had an open mic night on Thursday, and it was a huge success."

"It sounds like you're well on your way to having this store become the community hub that your sister dreamed of."

Anna didn't remember telling him about Bella being the inspiration for her shop, but then again, it wasn't exactly a secret. She was glad that word was traveling fast. It meant that people were talking about *Bella's Dream*.

"Velma told me about your sister. I'm sure she would be proud."

"Thanks, Todd." It always felt nice to hear that, even from a stranger.

"And if you should reach the point where you need a financial advisor, just say the word." Todd pulled out his business card and slid it across the counter.

"I will keep you in mind," Anna said. "But I need to make it through a full year in business before I know what I can afford to invest. I'm sure I will need to use some of my profits from the busy summer months to carry me through the winter."

"Fair enough," Todd said. "I'm here whenever you're ready."

After they finished chatting, Anna brought Todd's card into her office and stuck it inside a desk drawer. At some point she *should* probably think about her financial future. She was contributing every month to her retirement account, but if business stayed strong, she might also be able to have an additional investment portfolio.

However, that was a decision for another day.

Joe came in shortly after. Anna updated him on her conversation with Ellen, explaining that Charlie was holding Chris for questioning.

"That sounds like promising news. If Chris is guilty, Charlie will prove it," Joe said, with his usual confidence. "I'm just glad you're not getting yourself in the middle of this one."

Anna smiled. "Nope. But Ellen is keeping me posted." She decided not to mention that she *had* gotten involved until Charlie gave her and Ellen a firm talking-to.

"Glad to hear it," Joe said. Although, Anna wasn't quite convinced that Joe believed her.

Since her staff had the front of the store under control, Anna went back into her office to get some price quotes on renting a karaoke machine. Anna's initial research seemed to indicate that the best route would be to purchase a machine, rather than renting one. The equipment wasn't nearly as expensive as she thought, and this would allow her to have a karaoke night regularly without having to worry about renting equipment.

Anna didn't purchase it yet, because she wanted to ask around to make sure she got the best quality and bargain. But it was a start.

Just as Anna was about to close her computer, one of her employees knocked on her door. "I'm sorry to bother you Anna, but there is a customer who insists on speaking with you. She wouldn't say why but it can't be a complaint. She hasn't even ordered any ice cream yet."

Anna followed Trish into the dining room, and the young

woman gestured to the person who was waiting. It was Nina. She had dark circles under her eyes and was biting her nails.

Nina immediately stood up when Anna arrived.

"I'm sorry for stopping by unannounced, but I couldn't think of anyone else to turn to. I was afraid you wouldn't agree to meet with me if I called first. I desperately need your help."

Anna sat in the booth where Nina had been sitting and gestured for Nina to do the same. Anna was tempted to refuse to talk with her, since the only possible subject that Nina could want to discuss was Luke. But the distraught expression on Nina's face gave Anna pause. Even if it was a cautious pause.

"Just so you know, I'm not investigating Luke's murder anymore," Anna said. "Detective Doyle made Ellen and I promise that we would stop, and I don't have any intention of going back on my word."

"Please, hear me out," Nina pleaded. "I just left the police station. Detective Doyle asked me to come in and talk to him. Anna, he thinks Chris killed Luke. Chris was seen in a heated discussion with Luke a month before his death, and then Chris stopped by Luke's apartment the week before he was killed. Now, the police are convinced that Chris killed him."

"He was also caught breaking into Luke's apartment yesterday," Anna added.

"Oh, you heard about that, too."

"Yes. Ellen told me. Nina, I'm not going to lie. It doesn't look good for Chris. What makes you so sure that he's innocent?"

Nina clenched her fist. "I know my brother, and he *didn't* kill Luke."

"I understand how you feel, but I don't think that will be good enough for the police," Anna said. "They will need solid evidence, not just a sister's belief in her brother."

"I understand that. That's why I'm here. I need you to help me prove it."

"Nina, how on earth do you expect me to do that? As I said, I promised the police I'd stay out of it, and besides that, how would I go about proving that your brother is innocent? Does he even have an alibi?"

Nina hesitated. "No, he doesn't. But I *know* he's innocent."

"Then how do you explain all of the visits and the heated conversation between Luke and Chris? What did Chris want with Luke before he died, and why did he break into his apartment?"

Nina let out a deep breath. "That part I *do* know. I'm sure you know that when Luke and I dated, we were both addicts. Chris is the one who provided us with the drugs. We weren't the only ones. My brother sold drugs to a lot of people." Nina looked down. "Unfortunately, he still does. The reason Chris confronted Luke on Main Street that morning was because Chris somehow learned that Luke was having breakfast regularly with Detective Doyle. Chris was afraid that Luke was going to tell the police that he was dealing drugs. That's why their conversation got heated on Main Street that day. Chris also showed up at Luke's apartment before he died for the same reason. Luke assured him that he rarely even talked about his past life with the detective, and when he did, he focused on his own struggles. He didn't talk about others, and he didn't plan to. But Chris was paranoid."

"Nina, that information doesn't exactly help your brother. On the contrary, it gives him a motive."

"I'm worried about my brother for a lot of reasons. Chris may be a lot of things, but he is not a killer."

"You don't know that, Nina. He could very well have killed Luke because he thought he was going to get Charlie after him." Anna shivered as she thought of the brutal way in which Luke was killed. It would make sense that the killer was high. She couldn't imagine anybody in their right mind doing that to another person.

"I'm telling you, Anna, if they arrest Chris, they will have the wrong man, and the real killer will still be on the loose. There will be no justice for Luke or his family. I loved Luke, and I want to see his killer brought to justice, too. But I know it's not my brother. I understand that you're not convinced, but what if I can bring you solid evidence that Chris is innocent?"

"If you have evidence, why don't you bring it to the police?"

"I have to show you. Once you see, you'll understand. Meet me at my apartment tomorrow night, and I'll bring proof."

Anna shook her head. That sounded far too dangerous.

"Please, Anna. I'm begging you."

"I'll tell you what. I'll meet you in a public place. How about if we meet at the cove? There will be lots of people around. Can you bring your evidence there?"

"Okay," Nina said. "I'll do my best. Let's meet at 5:00. There should still be plenty of people at the beach."

Anna was counting on that.

CHAPTER 16

Business was steady on Sunday night and remained that way well into Monday.

When the afternoon rush on Monday died down, Anna needed a pick-me-up, so she headed over to *Cove Coffee* for an iced beverage.

Everyone in Seagull Cove must have had the same idea, because the line was practically out the door. As much as Anna hated to wait in line, she was pleased to see that business was also strong for Sonja.

Anna ordered a medium hazelnut iced coffee and a corn muffin. She glanced around the dining room for an empty table, but no such luck. She was about to take her order to go when someone called her name. She turned in the direction of the voice to find Jeremy Russo waving her over to his table.

"Why don't you join me?" he asked, gesturing to the empty chair on the other side of his table.

"Thanks," Anna said. "I had just given up hope of finding a table and didn't feel like going back to my shop."

"Seagull Cove can be wild during the summer months. It's

good for the local businesses, but for residents, it can be a bit inconvenient."

"I'm surprised to see you here in the middle of the afternoon. It must be a slow news day."

Jeremy smiled. "I just hit my deadline, so I'm taking a break. I worked through lunch, so I decided to come over here for a mid-afternoon snack."

"I'm pretty much doing the same thing, except that I didn't skip lunch. I just needed something to boost my energy."

"I admire your restraint in not turning to ice cream. That's totally what I'd be doing if I owned an ice cream parlor."

Anna chuckled. "That does happen more often than I care to admit. I have to limit myself." She took a sip of her coffee and savored its rich flavor.

"I heard that your open mic night was a success," Jeremy said.

"We had a great turnout. I think we're going to make it a regular event. Actually, you might be interested to know that Ruthie Valentino, the owner of *The Book Cove*, did a spectacular poetry reading. We're trying to convince her to publish some of her poems. If she does, that would make a great feature story for your newspaper. You know, book store owner turned author."

"Great. Now I can tell my boss that I *didn't* take a break. I can officially call this a work meeting," Jeremy said with a wink. "I'll keep my eyes open for Ruthie's book. By the way, have you done any further investigating since we last talked regarding your sister's accident?"

Anna let out a deep breath. "I've done a little research, but I've hit a brick wall."

"What do you mean?"

"The other night, I went through some old financial records that belonged to my sister. Shortly before her accident, she closed out her retirement account. I knew she had done that. She told me that she accumulated some credit card debt when we first started our counseling practice and weren't making a lot of money, so she wanted to pay that off. I didn't think too much of it at the time, but when I went through her credit card statements, there was no debt, and she never carried more than a small balance."

"Hmm, so, that, on top of the fact that Joe Wiggins might have seen her on the day of your grand opening, has you thinking that your instincts about her being alive is still a strong possibility."

"Exactly. Bella also withdrew the balance in her savings account shortly before her death, as well. Between the two accounts, there was a sizeable amount of money, and there is no trace of it."

Jeremy leaned back in his chair. "You said that you hit a wall. What did you mean?"

"The only person who Bella would potentially have confided in about her finances is her boyfriend, Grayson. But I don't want to tell him what I've learned. When Bella had her accident, Grayson was getting ready to propose. It took him forever to even *begin* to move on. If I'm wrong and tell him my suspicions, it could be harmful to his emotional well-being."

Jeremy looked thoughtfully at Anna.

"What would you do if you were me?" Anna asked.

"That's a tough one. But I do have some experience in trying to get information out of people without them realizing what I'm doing. You just moved to Seagull Cove, right?"

"I moved here in March. What does that have to do with anything?"

"If it were me, I'd tell Grayson that you came across some old paperwork and are trying to reconcile some things in your sister's finances before you dispose of the records. And then ask him if he knows anything about the accounts."

"Jeremy, you're a genius! I don't know why I didn't think of that."

Jeremy smiled playfully. "I wouldn't say I'm a genius. But *you* can if you'd like. I'm glad I could help."

"I've been meaning to reach out to Grayson anyway, just to check in and see how he's doing. It will be the perfect excuse. I can kill two birds with one stone."

"There you go." He smiled. "See? No more brick wall. My work here is done. I'd better get back to the newsroom before my editor realizes how long I've been gone. It was a pleasure speaking with you again. If you need to talk through anything else, you know where to find me."

"Thanks Jeremy. I might take you up on that."

By the time Jeremy left, the coffee line had died down. A tired-looking Sonja came over and sat where Jeremy had been sitting.

"I didn't know you knew Jeremy Russo. He's a great guy. And he's single, just in case you were wondering."

Anna leaned back in her chair and took the last sip of her iced coffee. "It's not like that between us. He's the journalist who covered my sister's boating accident. We were just catching up." At least that was *mostly* true. His dark hair and intense dark eyes gave him an aura of mystery that Anna couldn't help but find intriguing. Yet he also had a compassionate and friendly quality that made him approachable.

But the timing was all wrong. She didn't have the emotional energy to even think about beginning a relationship.

"That may be how you initially met him, but I saw the way he was looking at you. The two of you seemed to be enjoying one another's company."

"Don't be silly. We were discussing my sister. He was only being a kind and sympathetic journalist."

"Okay, Anna," Sonja said with a smirk before standing back up and wiping down the empty tables. "Whatever you say."

As Anna left, she glanced over at Sonja, who was still smirking as she cleaned. Anna shook her head as she left.

Main Street was packed with people, so Anna ducked into her office for some privacy and called Grayson.

"Hi, Anna," he replied, sounding surprised to hear from her. Just the sound of Grayson's voice made Anna miss Bella. She missed Grayson, too. Not only had Anna lost her sister, but as time went on, she realized that, because of Bella's accident, she also lost a man in her life whom she was certain would have made a wonderful brother-in-law.

"Hi, Grayson. It's great to hear your voice."

"You too, Anna."

"I was wondering if we could get together. I have a couple of questions that came up for me as I was going through some of Bella's things that I was hoping you might be able to answer. And besides, I've been meaning to reach out and see how you're doing. It's been far too long."

"Sure, it would be great to see you and to catch up. I don't know what questions I could possibly answer for you, but I'd be happy to try. Are you still working in Boston?"

"No, that's another thing. I moved to Seagull Cove in March. I closed the practice and opened an ice cream shop."

There were a few seconds of silence.

"Grayson?"

"Yes, I'm here. You just caught me by surprise. It's not too hard for you to be in Seagull Cove? I mean, the town where Bella died?"

"I don't think I could have done it even a couple of years ago. But I needed a change, and well, one thing led to another, and here I am. Besides, there are lots of warm memories of Bella here. I'm actually finding it kind of healing."

"I'm so happy to hear that. Bella would be thrilled. She always fantasized about opening an ice cream shop like the one you two used to go to in Boston. It sounds like we have a lot to catch up on. I could come to Seagull Cove on Sunday. Do you want me to meet you at your ice cream shop?"

Anna wasn't sure if Grayson had been back to Seagull Cove since the boating accident, and she was afraid it might be too much to process all at once if he saw that she had named the shop 'Bella's Dream.'"

"Why don't we meet at my house? I bought a cute little cottage a short distance from downtown. I'll make lunch and then we can walk over to the shop, and I'll show you around." This way, she could at least brace Grayson for seeing *Bella's Dream* for the first time. "I'll text you my address."

Now that they had made plans, Anna found herself looking forward to her lunch with Grayson on Sunday. It really *had* been too long.

What she wasn't looking forward to was her meeting with Nina that evening.

CHAPTER 17

When Anna returned to the front of the store, Joe was seated at the counter with his usual bowl of chocolate chip ice cream in front of him. She was about to fill him in on her conversation with Grayson when Olivia arrived for her first shift since her uncle's death. She looked more upbeat than the last couple of times Anna had seen her.

"Welcome back, Olivia," Anna said.

"Thanks. It feels good to be here. I don't think I could eat another casserole or handle any more visitors who want to talk about Uncle Luke. I don't mean to sound ungrateful. People have been awesome, and it's been comforting to be reminded of how many people loved him, but I'm ready to try to get my life back to normal."

"Well, there's been a steady flow of customers in here, so there should be plenty of activity to keep you busy." Anna glanced at her signature ice cream cone clock on the wall. "You're a little early. Did you forget that the second shift doesn't start until 5:00?"

"I know. I just needed to get out of the house. I was hoping you might need an extra person for the next couple of hours."

Anna was just about to tell Olivia to grab an apron and that they could always use the extra help when Alex jumped into the conversation. "You can finish my shift for me if you want. I wouldn't mind a couple of extra hours off."

"Thanks, Alex. Are you sure?"

"Absolutely," he said, pulling off his apron. "My friends are at the beach. I was going to join them after work, but I wouldn't mind getting there early."

"I guess that's settled then," Anna said.

Olivia got a fresh apron from the back and hopped behind the counter.

"There she is!" Joe said cheerfully, lifting up his bowl of ice cream so Olivia could wipe down the counter. "We missed you, kiddo."

Olivia smiled broadly. "I missed you guys, too. I didn't realize how much until just now. Although, I did at least get to see Anna a couple of times. She and my mom were working together until recently to try to find my uncle's killer."

Anna froze. That was *not* information that she wanted Joe to have. Now she was totally busted.

Joe turned his head in Anna's direction.

"I thought you told me that you and Ellen were *not* investigating," Joe said.

Olivia realized her blunder and mouthed 'sorry' to Anna.

"'Were' is the operative word in Olivia's sentence, Joe," Anna added as quickly as she could get the words out of her mouth. "Ellen heard how we found Marcus's killer last month and asked if I'd help her look into a few things."

"My mom pleaded with Anna," Olivia said, apparently

trying to undo the damage she had caused. "Anna didn't want to, but my mom begged until she finally gave in."

"Olivia is right. When I told you that I wasn't involved, I wasn't. Charlie had warned Ellen and me to stop. And we did. We've both decided to leave things to the police. Ellen is keeping me posted on what Charlie tells her, but we're no longer investigating."

Joe studied Anna, apparently trying to decide whether to believe her.

"I wouldn't lie to you, Joe." Anna felt a twinge of guilt, because she was walking a fine line. She was meeting with Nina in a couple of hours, so that could be interpreted as investigating. But she only agreed to meet with Nina to hear her out. She hadn't *technically* started investigating again. And she didn't have any plans to start up.

Joe simply nodded. Anna still had the feeling that he didn't believe her. Not that she could blame him.

At 5:00, the shop was still hopping with sunburned tourists, but Anna trusted her employees to handle things while she met with Nina. She was ready to get this over with, especially after her conversation with Joe.

Anna walked resolutely to the cove and across the sand to the jetty on the right side, where she and Nina had arranged to meet. Anna was surprised to see that Nina was accompanied by a man who she introduced as Scout. His shoulder length hair looked as if it hadn't been washed in the past week, and he was in dire need of a shave.

After a quick introduction, they hiked further out onto the rocks, where they could have a bit of privacy. Anna made sure they were out of earshot but in plain view of the dozens, if not hundreds, of beach-goers.

Nina and Scout sat on a rock, and Anna sat facing them. Scout, who wouldn't make direct eye contact with Anna, looked as if he wished he were anywhere but there.

"I don't have a lot of time. My employees are expecting me back in a few minutes," Anna said as an extra precaution, just so they knew that she would be missed before long.

"This won't take long," Nina said.

"You said that you had proof that Chris didn't kill Luke. Is Scout your proof?" Nina was wasting Anna's time if she thought Anna would take Scout's word on anything. "If Chris was with Scout at the time Luke was killed, he should just go to the police. I assume that's why you brought him here. To give your brother an alibi."

Nina couldn't possibly think that Anna was that naive.

"It's not that simple, Anna. Neither Chris or Scout want the police to know that they were together at the time of Luke's death." Nina turned to Scout. "Tell her what you told me."

"What I told you was that I didn't want to be here. What if Anna goes to the police?"

"If she does, you can deny everything, Scout. She doesn't have any proof to take to the police. Say what you have to say. There aren't any police here now. It would be your word against hers."

"Maybe. But I have a feeling they'd believe her and start investigating me. I don't need that kind of grief in my life."

"She won't, Scout. You promised you'd do it for Chris. You owe him. He covered for you, remember? Luke was good to you."

"Look, I don't have time for this," Anna said. She didn't want to be pulled into whatever scheme they had going on, and she certainly didn't trust either of them. Anna stood to leave.

"Wait," Nina said. "Just give us a couple of more minutes." She elbowed Scout.

"Fine. Chris was with me last Monday morning, when Luke was killed. The reason I won't go to the police to give him an alibi is because he was selling me drugs at the time."

Anna looked at Nina skeptically and shook her head. "You just said that Scout owes Chris a favor. He could just be saying this to provide a false alibi for Chris."

"I can prove it." Nina grabbed Scout's phone from his pocket and tapped a few times on the screen. Then she passed the phone to Anna. "You can read their exchange right there."

Anna skimmed through the texts, which consisted of Scout telling Chris that he needed drugs and Chris telling Scout to meet him at a location forty-five minutes away from Seagull Cove at 8:30 in the morning.

"See," Nina said. "Chris was with Scout at 8:30. He wasn't anywhere near Seagull Cove last Monday morning. He couldn't have killed Luke."

"This only proves they had plans to meet," Anna said. "How do I know they actually met? Chris could have blown off Scout and killed Luke. He could have sent these texts because he knew he'd need an alibi."

"If the police used the tracking device in Scout's phone, they'd find out they weren't anywhere near Seagull Cove when Luke was killed," Nina said. "But neither of these numb skulls will tell the police. And Chris won't betray Scout."

"Why don't they just track Chris's phone?" Anna asked.

"He left it at home on Monday morning, so it wouldn't

prove anything, except that his phone was at his house," Nina said.

"So, you're saying that Chris would go to jail for murder before he'd tell the truth to the police?" Anna asked. "If he's crazy enough to do that, then it's his choice."

"Detective Doyle thinks Chris is his man. My stupid brother thinks that he's going to be cleared as soon as the real killer is found."

"He's right," Anna said. "If your brother is innocent, the police will leave him alone when they find the real killer."

"People *do* go to jail for crimes they didn't commit. I don't want my brother to be one of those people," Nina said.

"I'm sorry, but I maintain my position. Chris has a choice. Face the music about his drug activity, or go to prison for murder. It's not up to me to help him, Nina."

Nina let out a deep breath. "While the police waste their time on my brother, the real killer is getting away with murder. I know that Luke's family wouldn't want that. Don't help me for my brother's sake. Do it for Luke's family. Chris isn't the only reason I want Luke's real killer behind bars. I loved Luke, and he deserves justice. How can I stay out of it when I know Luke's killer is still out there? We're on the same side, Anna. Just think about it."

Anna stood to leave. All she could think about was getting out of there and clearing her head. Nina could be right. Or she could be playing Anna.

"I'll think about it."

But Anna only said that because she wanted to leave. She had no intention of getting mixed up in this sordid situation.

CHAPTER 18

Anna tried to shake her conversation with Nina from her head, but she found herself replaying it as she walked back to *Bella's Dream*. If the police were chasing Chris and he wasn't the killer, then Nina was correct in saying that the real killer was going to get away with murder. However, Anna wasn't sure if she bought Scout's story. Nina's evidence of the text on Scout's phone was far from rock solid. For all Anna knew, Nina could have bribed Scout to vouch for Chris.

Nina should just go to the police with her evidence. It was true that her brother would get into trouble for dealing drugs, but it was better than a murder rap. Of course, it probably wasn't easy to turn in your own brother, even if it *was* in his best interest. Anna could see how the path of least resistance for Nina would be to convince Anna to investigate. *If* her story were true. That was a big "if."

Anna returned to *Bella's Dream* and immediately hopped behind the counter. She hoped that keeping busy would take her mind off Luke's murder. It was Charlie's job to sort this all out. Not Anna's. All Chris had to do was take responsibility for his actions, and he'd be cleared for murder. No. Anna wouldn't be touching that with a ten-foot pole.

The rest of the evening passed quickly. Anna smiled as she saw Olivia once again laughing with coworkers and customers. It was nice to see her taking her mind off her recent tragedy and smiling again.

By the end of the evening, Anna was looking forward to her walk home. The temperature had dropped into the seventies, and the air was crisp. When the wind blew in the right direction, the smell of fried food wafted through the air from a seafood restaurant down the street. When she got home, Anna sat on her front porch to enjoy the night air a little longer.

She was considering what she would make for lunch for Grayson's visit on Sunday when her phone pinged. It was Ellen.

I know it's late, but can we talk? The sooner the better.

Sure, Anna replied. *I'm just relaxing on my front porch. Call anytime in the next hour or so.*

In that case, would you mind if I came over for a few minutes? I need to get out of the house.

Anna texted Ellen her address, and within ten minutes, Ellen was climbing the wooden stairs of Anna's front porch.

"Come inside while I brew some tea," Anna said.

Anna brewed two large mugs of chamomile tea, and the women took their beverages onto the porch.

"Olivia seemed to have a great first day back at work," Anna said. "I think it's good for her to be back."

Ellen smiled. "I got that impression, too. I'm glad she's working at *Bella's Dream*. She enjoys it, and her coworkers have been very kind throughout this ordeal."

"I'm happy to hear that."

"But that's not why I came. Olivia didn't want me to breathe a word of this to you, so you can't tell her that I told you. But she saw you talking to Nina at the cove this afternoon when she was taking a walk during her break. Anna, are you back investigating Luke's murder?"

Anna let out a sharp breath. "I wasn't going to tell you about my conversation with Nina, because I didn't want to upset you. To answer your question, no. I'm not investigating again." Anna explained how Nina had shown up at *Bella's Dream* saying she had proof that Chris didn't kill Luke, and she relayed her earlier conversation with Nina and Scout.

Ellen listened with her mouth open. "So, you're saying that there is no way that Chris killed Luke?"

"I'm not saying that at all. Nina had proof that Chris was *supposed* to meet Scout at a location forty-five minutes away from Seagull Cove at the time that Luke was killed. But she can't prove that they actually *did* meet at that time. For all we know, Nina convinced Scout to give Luke a false alibi. The way I see it, if Chris was truly with Scout, all he needs to do to get himself off the hook for murder is to admit to being with Scout and to the reason why. Even if he is innocent of murder, he's still not willing to take the heat for purchasing drugs. I'm not going to risk my life investigating to clear someone who refuses to take responsibility for his own actions."

Ellen reflected for a moment. "On the other hand, if Nina and Scout *were* telling you the truth, then the police are wasting their time looking for evidence against Chris while the real killer is getting away with murdering my brother."

"That's also a possibility. But we promised Charlie that

we'd stay out of it. I think we should trust him to sort it all out."

"You could tell Charlie what you know," Ellen said.

"If you want me to, I will. I'm just not sure how much I trust Nina and Scout. They could be playing us in order to cause a distraction. I still think the best thing to do is to leave the investigating to Charlie."

There was a long silence. "That's not the only reason I'm here," Ellen said. "I had dinner with Nicole, and she told me that when she was going through Luke's business records, she came across a note in Luke's handwriting." Ellen pulled her phone from her purse, tapped a few times, and slid it over to Anna. "Here it is."

It was a photo of a note that said, "Proof of arson. Talk to Philip about new evidence."

"It was stuck in between a pile of papers that was dated a couple of days before Luke's death. Nicole searched Luke's office to try to find the evidence Luke was referring to, but she was unsuccessful. She brought the original note to the police."

Anna let out a deep sigh. "Do you realize what this means?"

Ellen nodded. "There is a decent chance that Chris has an alibi, and we now know that Luke had some type of proof that Philip started the fire at his own house. If that's the case, Philip's motive is stronger than ever."

"This means that Luke might have confronted Philip about the arson and accused him of setting his house on fire, and then, a couple of days later, Luke was found murdered. And now, the police are fixated on Chris. I don't like this one bit," Anna said.

"Of course, we have no way of knowing if Luke actually *did* talk to Philip. But there's one more thing. When Nicole brought the note to the police, Charlie told her that Philip's alibi turned out to be false."

"I thought it was kind of flimsy from the beginning. Philip said he was having breakfast with a friend," Anna said.

"Charlie didn't elaborate, but I'm guessing Philip's friend wouldn't confirm his story."

"That's good news, then. Between the note and Philip no longer having an alibi, I'm sure the police will look into it."

"I wish that were the case. Nicole also told me that Charlie took the note from her, but he didn't seem as interested in Philip as Nicole had hoped. She said that Charlie still seemed fixated on proving that Chris is guilty. And since he is the only detective in town, he has to prioritize his time. What if Nina was telling you the truth? Philip could have killed Luke, and now he is roaming free because the police are determined to prove that Chris is the guilty one."

"It sounds like you think we should reopen our investigation," Anna said.

Ellen shrugged. "I think we should consider it."

CHAPTER 19

Anna tossed and turned all night on Monday, with Ellen's suggestion of reopening their investigation swirling around in her mind. By the time she poured her coffee and sliced a banana onto her morning corn flakes, she had waffled back and forth several times.

Ellen had brought her some compelling information the previous evening. Philip's alibi had fallen through, and Luke had apparently planned to confront him about the fire. It was an awfully big coincidence that Luke was murdered shortly after. Perhaps too large to be a coincidence. Yet Charlie seemed fixated on Chris, who refused to come forward with his alibi.

But the thought of the grief Joe would give her if she and Ellen decided to resume their investigation was reason enough to let it go.

There was no doubt about it. This was what her mother called "stuck between a rock and a hard place."

It wasn't until she had washed the breakfast dishes and

taken her shower that Anna had made up her mind. The idea of Philip literally getting away with murder was just too much. No matter how ridiculous and self-sabotaging Chris was being, she couldn't stand by and do nothing while Chris may be taking the blame for Philip's actions. Luke deserved justice, and so did Ellen and Olivia.

She texted Ellen before she could change her mind again. *I'm in. Let's reopen our investigation and find Luke's killer once and for all.*

I was hoping you'd say that. I'll stop by later and we can plan our next move.

It was another busy day in the shop, which always made Anna feel more optimistic about life in general. By now, *Bella's Dream* was beginning to run like a well-oiled machine. When Ellen popped in at 1:00, Anna was easily able to take off for a while.

"Do you want to grab a coffee while we talk?" Ellen asked. "I could use some caffeine."

"Sounds great," Anna said.

The women walked a few doors up the street to *Cove Coffee*, ordered their beverages, and claimed the last open table.

"I was glad to hear that you wanted to start investigating again," Ellen said.

"I've been agonizing over the decision since we talked last night, but in the end, it's the right thing to do. We just have to be extremely careful that neither Charlie Doyle or Joe Wiggins discover what we're doing, or I'll never hear the end of it," Anna said.

"Understood. Caleb wouldn't be too pleased if he knew what I was up to, either. As far as anyone is concerned, we bonded over the fact that we both tragically lost a sibling, and that's why we're spending so much time together," Ellen said.

"I suppose there's some truth to that. That's what made me want to help you to begin with."

"So, what do you think our next move should be?" Ellen asked.

"We need to learn as much as we can about Philip. If Luke had proof that he burned down his house thinking he would collect insurance money, that would be the strongest motive that we've encountered yet."

"Agreed. Why don't we talk to Nicole again and see what she can tell us? She went back to work this week, so I'll have to see when she is available. Then we can go from there."

"Let's do it," Anna said.

"I'll come back to *Bella's Dream* with you. I want to say hello to Olivia and maybe get myself an ice cream cone. I saw a customer walk out with a couple of scoops of rocky road, and I can't get it out of my head."

Anna chuckled. "That's the story of my life. I thought I'd get used to being around ice cream all day and be less tempted, but that has not turned out to be the case. It takes all my willpower to not overindulge. Some days I lose the battle."

Ellen ordered her ice cream, and her daughter proudly served it to her in the dining room. Olivia was due for a break, so she sat down with her mother for a few minutes and had a scoop of her own.

Just as Ellen was about to leave, Nina came into the shop. The woman looked fit to be tied. She made a beeline for Anna and pointed her index finger into Anna's face. "You told the police about Chris selling drugs to Scout."

"Nina, please lower your voice," Anna said, taking a step back. "There are customers in the shop."

Nina glanced around, but fortunately, everyone was so absorbed in their own conversations and ice cream that nobody seemed to be paying attention. Nina lowered her voice to a whisper. "It *had* to be you. We didn't tell anyone else."

Out of the corner of her eye, Anna saw Ellen motion for Olivia to get back to work. Olivia scooted behind the counter. When Anna noticed Ellen and Olivia, her cheeks turned red. Anna escorted Nina into her office with Ellen following close behind them.

Anna sat behind her desk, and Ellen and Nina took the chairs across from her.

"I'm sorry. I hope I didn't upset Olivia. I didn't realize the two of you were in here," Nina said to Ellen. "I trust that Anna filled you in on our conversation yesterday."

"She did."

"As Scout and I were headed back to my car, we had the sense someone was following us. Scout searched around, but he couldn't find anyone. He called me this morning and said that he had the same feeling for the rest of the evening, while he was out with his friends. Then, a couple of hours ago, Charlie came and arrested Scout and Chris for possession of drugs. Of course, he doesn't have any evidence to charge Chris with murder, but someone was following us, and it can't be a coincidence that Charlie arrested them just after we talked to Anna. The police must have been following us. How could you do that, Anna? I came to you for help. I trusted you. I know my brother has gotten into a lot of trouble. I have too, for that matter. But I got help, and I know Chris will, too." Tears fell down Nina's face. "All I want is for my brother to have a fighting chance and for Luke's killer to be found. My brother didn't do it."

Anna glanced over at Ellen, wondering how she would react to Nina's outburst.

Ellen was looking at Nina with compassion. She took Nina's hand. "Nina, I know all too well what it feels like to have a brother who is making all the wrong choices. But I can assure you, Anna didn't go to the police with what you told her. In fact, we talked last night, and we decided to start investigating again. If the police were following Chris and Scout, it wasn't because Anna told them anything."

Nina brightened up. "You mean you believe that Chris is innocent?"

"We think there is enough evidence to continue investigating. We believe there's a good chance that Chris didn't do it."

Nina breathed a sigh of relief. "That's good enough for me. I promise you won't regret your decision. Ellen, I know that you aren't my biggest fan, and I understand why. I was not the best version of myself when I dated Luke. Not even close. But I'm working on it, and I *did* love your brother. I want his killer to be behind bars, too."

Ellen squeezed Nina's hand. "I believe you."

And Anna did, too. At least she believed that Nina *thought* her brother was innocent. It was still possible that Chris was guilty.

"So, if we assume that Chris didn't kill Luke, who do you think did?" Anna asked Nina.

"I wish I knew. I don't know much about Luke's present

life. I mean, his life before he died. I wish I could be more helpful on that front. All I know is that my brother didn't do it and I can't think of anyone who knew Luke while I was dating him who would have a motive to kill him. I think it must be someone he met after we broke up."

Anna agreed. "It's beginning to look that way. If you think of anyone at all, please let us know."

Nina stood to leave. "I will. And if there's anything else I can do, don't hesitate to ask."

"Do you think we can really rule Chris out?" Ellen asked after Nina left.

"He does have an alibi. It's not rock solid, because there's always the chance that Scout could be lying to cover for him. But either way, I don't think we should focus on Chris. The police are doing that. The best use of our time is to pursue other avenues."

"Our other suspects, before we stopped investigating, were Nina, Wil, Philip, and Loni," Ellen said.

"I think it's safe to say that Nina didn't do it. It's unlikely that she would be begging us to investigate if she were."

"Agreed. Loni doesn't have much of a motive, either," Ellen said.

"We should focus our attention on Philip. He has the strongest motive, and we know that Luke planned to confront him with evidence of arson. And I would like to find out what happened between Wil and Luke. That will allow us to either rule out Wil, or, if whatever took place between them could be a motive for murder, keep him on our list of suspects," Anna said.

"I'll work on that. Wil clearly didn't want to tell me what

happened when we talked to him at my house last week, but maybe Danielle will tell me."

"And I'll try to come up with a way to get more information about Philip. I wish I could ask Joe. I'm sure he'd know what to do."

CHAPTER 20

Wednesday, Thursday, and Friday were relatively uneventful. Sunburned tourists, as well as many of the town's residents, continued to keep *Bella's Dream* alive with activity, so Anna spent most of the days and evenings assisting behind the counter when the line grew particularly long.

Ellen hadn't been in touch since Tuesday, but Anna assumed that it was because she was busy, now that her schedule was getting back to normal.

Meanwhile, Anna continued to mull the mystery of Luke's murder around in the back of her mind.

On Saturday morning before the store opened, Anna was having a cup of coffee in the dining room of her shop when Ellen tapped on the window.

Anna unlocked the front door and let her in.

"Hi, Anna, I was hoping you'd be here early. I had to run an errand in town, but I wanted to touch base."

"I brewed a fresh pot of coffee. Can I get you a cup?"

"No, thanks. I need to get home. I just wanted to tell you

that I haven't forgotten about our plans to continue the investigation. It's just been harder than I thought it would to get back into the swing of things after Luke's death, so I've been moving slowly. I finally finished cleaning out his apartment."

"I figured you must be busy."

"I did run into Charlie Doyle last night and got the whole story about Philip's alibi falling through. Apparently, Philip thought his friend would cover for him, but when the police went to verify his alibi with his friend, he wouldn't. He admitted that Philip was not with him at the time of Luke's death, as Philip had previously claimed. I don't trust Philip at all."

"He does seem pretty cocky. Can you imagine asking a friend to lie to the police on your behalf? Serves him right. Have you had any luck finding out what happened between Wil and Luke?"

Ellen shook her head. "Not yet. I talked with Wil's wife, Danielle, to see if she'd be willing to tell me, but she said that it was up to Wil to make that decision."

"I suppose she's right," Anna said.

"She did agree to encourage him to talk to me, but she maintained that the decision should be Wil's. I'm hoping that he will choose to confide in me. Time will tell."

"If Wil is guilty, he may not have even told Danielle the truth," Anna said. "The more I think about it, until we find out what happened between them, Wil is still a suspect as far as I'm concerned. They clearly had a rocky history, and then they had another falling out just before Luke died. It could be irrelevant, but it also could be a motive for murder."

"Agreed," Ellen said. "I'll let you know if I hear from him."

Despite a busy day on Saturday, Anna went home once she

got her evening employees settled in for their shift. Since Grayson was coming for lunch the following afternoon, she wanted to clean her cottage and go grocery shopping. Grayson's visit was a good excuse to give her home a thorough cleaning. That way, after Mass the following morning, all she would have to do was pick up some fresh bread and prepare lunch.

She went to an early Mass at Holy Family Church on Sunday so she would have plenty of time to leisurely make lunch and tend to her garden. She needed to be in the right frame of mind when she met with Grayson. It would likely be emotional to see him, and make her miss her sister all the more. Anna was watering her garden and mentally preparing to see Grayson, when Ellen called.

"I just spoke with Danielle. She wants me to meet her and Wil at *Cove Coffee* in a half hour. I know it's last minute, but can you join us?"

Anna looked at the clock on her stove. She had two hours before Grayson was due to arrive. Maybe it wouldn't be a bad idea to keep busy after all and not over-prepare.

"Okay, I'll meet you there in a half hour. But if it goes any longer than an hour, I have to leave. I have a friend coming over for lunch."

When Anna arrived at *Cove Coffee*, Ellen, Wil, and Danielle were already there. Wil and Danielle seemed a little put off that Anna was there. Anna, too, felt as though she were intruding, but there was no other way to be present. She had already invested too much time and energy into this case to step back now.

Ellen acted as though Anna's presence was the most natural thing in the world, and Anna followed her lead.

Wil started the conversation by addressing Ellen. "Danielle and I were talking last night, and we thought you had a right to know what happened between Luke and me. I didn't want to tell you at first, because I thought it might tarnish Luke's memory, but since you asked about it again, I figured it was important to you."

"Did Luke tell you anything about the reason why Wil and I separated?" Danielle asked.

Ellen shook her head. "Not that I recall."

Wil let out a sharp breath. "I didn't think so. A couple of years ago, I made some bad business decisions, and I was in a bit of a financial bind. It was at that time that Luke and Nina came to my house and asked to borrow money. Of course, even if I had it, I wouldn't have given it to them because I knew they would only use it to buy drugs. But I truly didn't have any money to spare at that point, anyway."

"That was the night that Luke and Nina stole your credit card," Ellen said.

"Yes. I realized that my credit card was missing the following day and was able to cancel it before they could do too much damage. But what I didn't realize at the time was that Luke had also stolen my wife's diamond necklace."

Ellen gasped. "I'm so sorry. If I had known, I would have replaced it."

"It wasn't your fault," Danielle said. "We don't want you to feel that way. It wasn't your responsibility to replace it. But I was devastated. In addition to having monetary value, the necklace had been passed down to me from my grandmother and couldn't be replaced, anyway."

Ellen looked as if she were about to cry.

"This is why Wil didn't want to tell you. He didn't want to hurt you unnecessarily," Danielle said.

Wil continued. "Shortly after that incident, I borrowed some money from a friend and was able to get my business back on track. I was gradually able to pay off my debts, and things got much better as more money started coming in."

"I still don't understand what changed between you and Luke in the weeks before he died. It seemed like you had forgiven him for everything that had happened that night. What changed?" Ellen asked.

"I'm getting to that. Danielle only wore that necklace on special occasions, so it wasn't until six months after Luke and Nina came to our house to ask for money that Danielle realized the necklace was missing."

"I'm ashamed to say it now," Danielle said, "but when I thought back on how much debt Wil was in, and how he suddenly came up with enough money to get his business back on track, I assumed that he must have sold my necklace. He told me he borrowed the money from his friend, and his friend confirmed his story, but I didn't believe them."

"Is that why the two of you separated for a while?" Ellen asked.

"We were already having some problems in our marriage before then, but that was the straw that broke the camel's back," Danielle said.

"But you're back together now," Ellen observed. "I'm so happy about that."

They both smiled.

"Thank you," Wil said. "We owe that to Luke. He finally worked up the courage to tell me about the necklace a couple of weeks before he died. As soon as he got clean and moved back to Seagull Cove, Luke apologized about the credit card. He even insisted on paying me back for the items he charged. But it took him a little longer to come clean about the necklace, because he knew that it was irreplaceable."

"And that's when you and Luke stopped talking again," Ellen said.

"I was furious, both because he stole an irreplaceable necklace and because it caused my wife and I to separate," Wil said. "We were heading towards a divorce when Luke told me. It wasn't until he told Danielle the whole story that she agreed to try to work things out."

"I felt awful that I didn't believe Wil." Danielle smiled at her husband. "And I missed him terribly. It's just that I didn't trust him anymore. As soon as Luke told me what happened, Wil moved back into our home, and we are committed to repairing our marriage."

"Ellen, I want you to know that I didn't stay angry at Luke for long," Wil said. "Two Sundays ago, the day before Luke died, Danielle and I went to Luke's house and told him that we forgave him for everything. We were just happy that the truth was out. We even took him to the *Sand Dollar Grille* for lunch to prove that all was forgiven."

"It was a wonderful afternoon," Danielle said. "We spent it reminiscing over old times and talking about our futures. Luke really loved Nicole, as well as his job. His future was so bright." Danielle's eyes filled with tears. "I am so happy we didn't put off that conversation, and that we all made our peace before he died."

Tears spilled from Ellen's eyes. "Thank you for being such good friends to my brother. He loved you both very much."

"We loved him, too. The man who stole from us that one

night wasn't Luke as far as we're concerned. We prefer to remember all the good things he did for us. He introduced the two of us, after all."

"I forgot about that," Ellen said.

Anna just listened as the three of them talked, feeling privileged to witness such a beautiful moment.

After Wil and Danielle left the coffee shop, Anna gave Ellen a hug. "I'm glad it didn't turn out to be Wil. I believed their story one hundred percent."

"I did, too," Ellen said. "If Wil were guilty, Danielle wouldn't be helping him cover by making up that story. But just to be safe, I'll verify it with Raymond, who owns the *Sand Dollar Grille*. He's always there, so he probably saw them."

"That's not a bad idea, although, as you said, it's probably not necessary." Anna glanced at the clock. "It's been nearly an hour. I'd better get back home for my lunch guest."

"Thanks again, Anna. We'll talk soon."

CHAPTER 21

After their conversation with Wil and Danielle, Anna went home to prepare her new favorite lunch for herself and Grayson.

She cut four slices of fresh bread and spread some oil and vinegar on them. She placed some fresh mozzarella cheese, along with a generous helping of fresh basil. Then she sliced an early-ripened tomato from her garden and added it to the sandwiches. She also scooped some homemade potato salad, which she had prepared the night before, onto their plates.

Once lunch was prepared, Anna picked some leaves from her mint plant and added it to the fresh brewed iced tea, which she had also made the night before. Just as she finished, Grayson arrived in a beige Audi convertible. He had the same clean-cut haircut that he had worn since he dated Bella, although it appeared a bit disheveled from his ride in the convertible. He wore navy slacks and a white polo shirt and carried a bottle of Anna's favorite red wine.

Anna became choked up, as she always did when she saw Grayson. Something deep inside her half-expected Bella to pop out of the passenger seat, with her long red hair blowing in the wind while wearing that infectious smile. Anna tried to swallow the lump in her throat. Judging from Grayson's expression, seeing Anna was causing similar feelings to surface in him.

Anna thought of all the bittersweet memories she and Grayson shared together with Bella and their friends.

Grayson and Bella had met at a college reunion. They both attended the same school but had never met until their fifteenth class reunion. From that day on, they had been inseparable.

As hard as it was to see Grayson, her heart also swelled with joy. Anna felt a special bond with him, because among all their friends, the two of them had shared the greatest loss. Anna would never forget the night before Bella's funeral, when they had taken a walk together, and Grayson showed Anna the ring he had purchased for Bella. He had been planning to propose two months later, at Christmas.

She hugged Grayson and took the bottle that he offered her.

"It's wonderful to see you," she managed to say with great emotion in her voice.

"You too, Anna. Until I heard your voice on the phone the other day, I hadn't realized that so much time had passed."

"Me, too."

"I still miss Bella so much," Grayson said.

Anna squeezed his forearm. "I do, too. I can't even tell you. They say time heals all wounds, but I don't think that's true. I'm still waiting." Despite Anna's best efforts, a tear streamed down her cheek. "I'm sorry. I didn't mean for this to be a sad reunion." Anna looped her arm through Grayson's. "Come on,

I prepared a nice lunch. Then, I want to show you my ice cream shop."

Anna led Grayson through the gate of her white picket fence and down the cement walkway, leading to her front porch.

Grayson paused to admire Anna's home. "I love your cottage. Bella would have loved this, too." Then he took in the small English garden and pony cart planter with wisps of colorful flowers sprouting up. "Wait, wasn't Bella always teasing you because you had a black thumb?"

Anna chuckled. "Good memory. Fortunately, I had the help of a kind neighbor, who taught me how to plant an English garden last month in exchange for ice cream."

"Sounds like you got a good deal."

"For sure," Anna said.

As they climbed the steps, Wanda awkwardly stood up with a handful of weeds in hand. Anna had been so lost in her own thoughts that she hadn't realized that Wanda was there.

Wanda waved awkwardly as she threw the weeds into a nearby barrel, then bent over and continued weeding.

Anna led Grayson inside. She opened the bottle of red wine that he brought and poured two glasses, along with two glasses of cold water, since it was a hot day. They said grace together, and dug in.

"Judging from your car, it looks like you are doing well," Anna said.

Grayson had been working hard on a startup, which was just getting off the ground, when Bella passed away.

"Business is good. I can't complain."

Bella had been a free spirit, while Grayson was more serious and business-minded. They had made a good pair.

Grayson caught Anna up on his business and his parents, and Anna caught Grayson up on her family, especially Sophia, her sixteen-year-old niece.

"So, you said you had some questions about Bella that you wanted to ask me," Grayson said when they exhausted the topic of their families. "I can't imagine what I could tell you after all this time that you wouldn't already know. Bella was pretty much an open book, especially with you."

"When I moved into this cottage, I took with me the financial records from our business, as well as Bella's personal files, which I had in my storage bin at my condo in Boston. I hadn't really gone through Bella's personal files, except to do what I needed to close out her affairs. As I was unpacking the boxes, I took a look through some of the files and saw a few things that didn't make sense. I just want to make sure that Bella didn't have any accounts that we weren't aware of. In particular, a retirement account. Did she ever mention anything about that to you?"

Grayson thought for a moment. "Not that I recall. We didn't have many conversations about finances. To be honest, I don't even know if she had a retirement account. But I'm sure that if she did, the statements would have been sent to you after her death. Didn't you have the mail from her apartment forwarded to you?"

"Yes, but it was such a tumultuous time that some of the details are foggy. If there was a retirement account, I imagine that the statements would have been forwarded to me. But as I was unpacking her boxes, I thought I remembered her telling me that she had one, and I didn't see any statements. But now that I think about it, she might have said that she planned to *start* one."

Anna hoped that Grayson was buying her mixed-up story. She hated being so secretive, even if it was for his own good. He seemed happier than she had seen him in a long time, and she guessed that he was finally moving forward with his life. The last thing she wanted was to give him false hope. This was the only way to get the information from Grayson without telling him about her suspicions that Bella might still be alive. However, it turned out that Anna wasn't learning anything that she didn't already know.

"The only thing I remember about Bella's finances was that she prided herself on not carrying any credit card debt. I only remember, because I'm the same way, and that was something that I admired about Bella."

"You're right about that," Anna said. "For someone who was impulsive by nature, she always handled her finances well and didn't tend to buy things unless she could afford to pay cash for them."

Still, this was nothing that Anna didn't already know, except that it further confirmed her suspicions that Bella never had any substantial credit card debt.

"I also admired how thrifty Bella was," Grayson continued. "For example, the summer before she died, Bella wanted to get back into swimming shape." He smiled nostalgically. "She was unwilling to pay for an expensive membership for a gym with a pool, so she drove three times a week to Revere Beach and swam laps along the shoreline."

Anna smiled. "Yes, that does sound like Bella." As those words were coming out of Anna's mouth, she realized something. "Wait a minute! Bella started swimming the summer before her boating accident?"

Grayson nodded. "She said that it was one of her favorite

ways to get into shape and that she didn't feel she was active enough sitting and talking to clients all day."

That was odd. Why hadn't Bella told Anna she was swimming again?

"I thought she was working out at a gym in Boston," Anna said.

Grayson shook his head. "She told me she canceled her membership."

Anna knew that wasn't true. She distinctly remembered that Bella worked out on her lunch break at a nearby gym in Boston. She specifically didn't schedule clients for an hour and a half, so she could get in a workout and a quick shower. She even ate lunch at her desk so she would have enough time for a workout.

Anna decided not to mention that. "Bella was on the swim team in high school. We both loved to swim," she said instead.

Grayson smiled and looked as if he were a million miles away. "I loved Bella's free spirit. She was always surprising me. Did you know that the summer before she died, she took a course on how to give manicures and pedicures? Just out of the blue like that," he said, snapping his fingers. "She said not to tell anyone. I don't know why, but of course, I don't think she'd mind that I told you now."

"That *is* strange. Maybe she wanted to save money by learning to do them herself."

Grayson chuckled. "Maybe. That would make sense, because she wasn't planning to take the licensing exam at the end of the course. She just wanted to learn how to do it."

Or perhaps Bella was looking for a new career to fall back on after she assumed a new identity. If she had planned to use a new name, she would need to take the exam under that new name, and in whatever state where she eventually settled. Anna wasn't sure how it all worked, but she would definitely be researching that.

"So, are you going to show me this ice cream shop of yours?" Grayson asked.

"Before I take you there, I need to tell you something about it." Anna filled Grayson in on her motivation for opening the shop and that she had named it in honor of her sister. "I just wanted you to know this beforehand, so it wasn't a shock."

"I appreciate that. And it is a beautiful gesture. Bella would have loved it."

They took Grayson's car to *Bella's Dream,* and Anna introduced him to Velma and her other employees, as well as to Joe Wiggins.

After a tour and an ice cream for dessert, Grayson left. They both promised they wouldn't let so much time pass before another visit, but given how bittersweet it was to see each other, Anna wondered if they both meant it.

CHAPTER 22

When Grayson left, Joe had just finished his ice cream and was getting ready to leave.

"I'm guessing that you decided to tell Grayson about your suspicions," he said.

Anna led Joe to an empty booth where they could talk in private.

"Not exactly," she said as they sat down.

"I don't understand," Joe said. "Do you mean that it's just a coincidence that you had lunch with Grayson at the same time that you've been looking into your sister's death again?"

"No. I ran into Jeremy Russo at *Cove Coffee* the other day and told him about my dilemma of wanting to ask Grayson some questions about my sister, but at the same time, not wanting to tell him about my suspicions that she might still be alive. Jeremy gave me the idea of telling Grayson that I came across some of Bella's files while I was moving and that I had a few questions that I thought he might be able to answer."

"And did you discover any useful information?"

"Not about Bella's retirement account or any potential

credit card debt, as I'd hoped. It turns out that he didn't know much about her finances. But I learned a couple of other really interesting things."

Joe waited for Anna to continue.

"First, Grayson told me that in the months leading up to the accident, Bella had been doing some swim training. He said she would train at the beach, because she didn't want to pay for an expensive gym membership just to have access to a pool."

"Was that unusual for Bella? Was that how she stayed in shape?"

"Yes and no. We were both swimmers in high school, but, more recently, Bella had been going to a gym in Boston during her lunch break. And that's not all. Grayson said that Bella was taking classes to learn how to become a nail technician. Bella told Grayson that she was just taking classes so she could learn how to give herself better manicures and pedicures and to save money, but why wouldn't she have mentioned that to me? And besides, who does that? Those courses probably cost more than dozens of manicures and pedicures."

"What do you think it means?" Joe asked.

Anna let out a deep breath. "All of Bella's professional training was in psychological counseling, so if she were going to fake her death and assume a new identity, she would need a trade to fall back on. Her licenses are under her real name, so she couldn't use those. I think it's possible that she was trying to get a head start on a new profession. I mean, she could have lived off her retirement money while she finished her training and took the exams. I assume she'd need to get her license in whatever state she was planning to move to, and in whatever new name she is using."

Joe gazed out the floor-to-ceiling window that made up much of her dining room wall.

"What are you thinking?" Anna finally asked.

"It's a tough one, Anna. Every bit of evidence that we've discovered that points to your sister still being alive is circumstantial - my seeing someone who looks like her, the location of the boat crash being close to land, Bella closing out her retirement and savings accounts and claiming that she has credit card debt, the swim training, and the nail technician classes."

"That's true. But, Joe, you have to admit that the circumstantial evidence is starting to pile up."

"I can't deny that. But you still don't have any leads on what to do next. If Bella is, in fact, alive, you have no idea where she could be. And more importantly, you have no idea why she faked her death. If she wants her family to believe she is dead, she must have a compelling reason."

"That's true. I have no idea what my next step will be. But if nothing else, I am more convinced than ever that I need to do *something*."

Since everything was running smoothly in the shop, Anna decided to take the entire day off, rather than coming to work after her lunch with Grayson, as she had planned. She needed to decompress.

After returning home, she made herself some lemonade and took it to her front porch. After a few moments, she noticed that Wanda was also sitting on her own front porch.

"Your garden seems to be thriving," Wanda said.

Anna smiled. "You sound surprised."

"Well, you're the one who said you had a black thumb."

"I think I just needed the right teacher."

"Perhaps. It's certainly improved the view from my living room a good bit."

"I'm happy to hear that."

Anna had the feeling that Wanda wanted to say something else. She wasn't usually one to make small talk unless she had an ulterior motive.

"Would you like to take a closer look?" Anna asked.

Wanda got up and walked around to Anna's front gate, making her way into Anna's yard. Her long grey hair was tied back in a ponytail. Anna observed Wanda while she made her way over. She was tall and thin, and her skin was smooth and youthful. With a more stylish haircut, she would look younger than her sixty years, rather than older, as she did now. Anna knew Wanda was about sixty, because Joe and Velma had told her that they had been in the same grade growing up.

Wanda examined the garden like a professor who was about to give Anna a grade. "It looks healthy. We haven't had a heat wave yet, but we likely will in August. If that happens, you'll want to water everything twice a day."

"That's good to know," Anna said.

Wanda paused, as if she wanted to say something else. "Daniel tells me that you saw him on the porch when you were walking along Mile Long Beach a couple of weeks ago. I appreciate that you didn't ask any personal questions, like why I don't live there with my husband anymore." So, Wanda *had* lived there with Daniel at some point.

"Of course not," Anna said. "That's your business."

Wanda looked down. "I appreciate that. That's why I'm not

going to ask you about that handsome gentleman caller you had for lunch today."

Anna suppressed a chuckle. So, *that's* what Wanda wanted. She was curious to know more about Grayson.

"But I couldn't help but overhear you talking about your sister, and I don't think I ever expressed my condolences. I mean, I know she died before you moved here, but I wanted to tell you how sorry I am, anyway. It's awful to lose a loved one at any age, but it's worse when the person is so young. It's just not fair."

Wanda tried to hide the wave of emotion that came across her, but it spilled into her voice and onto her face. Anna knew from experience that often when people presented themselves as stoic and emotionless, it was often because it was the only way they knew how to keep the floodgates from opening.

"Thank you. And you're right. It's not fair at all. Bella was my Irish twin sister. She was eleven months younger than me and died in a tragic boating accident four years ago, in the waters right off Seagull Cove."

Wanda thought for a moment. "I'm sorry, Anna. I think I remember reading about that in the newspaper. I didn't realize that woman was your sister."

Anna nodded. "Grayson was Bella's boyfriend. We haven't talked in a while, so I invited him over for lunch to catch up. It was good to see Grayson, but at the same time it was hard. I guess you could say it was bittersweet."

"I understand." Wanda didn't say anything else, although Anna had a feeling she was tempted to. Anna could practically feel the emotion swirling around in Wanda's heart, but she was afraid that if she pushed Wanda, it would damage their fragile friendship.

"Can I pour you some lemonade?" Anna ventured instead. "I have plenty."

"Oh, thank you, but I really have some chores to finish up inside. I need to straighten up. Daniel's coming for supper," she said, dashing off.

Wanda, along with her unconventional relationship with her husband, certainly was a mystery. It was one that Anna hoped would reveal itself as time went on.

CHAPTER 23

After taking Sunday off, Anna awoke surprisingly refreshed on Monday morning. She hadn't realized how much she needed some time away from the shop. She promised herself she would do that more often, even during the busy summer season.

Just before Anna opened *Bella's Dream,* Ellen called to let her know that she and Caleb stopped by the *Sand Dollar Grille* to talk with the owner, Raymond, and he verified Wil's and Danielle's story. They had, indeed, been at the restaurant the day before Luke's death, and from Ray's perspective, the three seemed to be having a grand old time, with lots of laughter and happy chatter."

"I'm so glad to hear that," Anna said. "I know how devastated you would have been if Wil turned out to be the killer. I guess we should get to work trying to learn more about Philip."

"Considering Nicole found that note in Luke's files about the arson, that makes the most sense."

Anna agreed. "There's something about Philip that I don't

trust. He's the one who told Charlie that we had been investigating. It's as if he wanted to stop us from looking into things. I think he's hiding something."

"We can't exactly stop by his house to talk to him again," Ellen said.

"Definitely not. He'd go squealing to Charlie again in a heartbeat, and we'd be in even bigger trouble this time. Why don't we both mull it over and try to come up with our next move? I haven't had much time to think about it since we talked yesterday."

"Me, either," Ellen said. "We'll talk soon."

Before opening *Bella's Dream*, Anna went to *Cove Coffee* for her morning caffeine fix. She took her drink to an outdoor table where Sonja, the owner, joined her. "It's been a crazy-busy morning. I could use a break."

"I don't envy your having to open the shop so early every morning," Anna said. "That's the nice thing about owning an ice cream shop. People aren't usually in the mood for sweets until after 11:00. Of course, I imagine your business will be more consistent than mine during the colder winter months."

"And I get to close up shop a few hours earlier than you do," Sonja added with a wink.

"Good point. I find I don't have as much of a social life since I've opened *Bella's Dream*. And being in a new town, I don't live close to my friends anymore." The truth was, so much of Anna's social life had included Bella that after her death, Anna had tended to withdraw and never really got back into the swing of things when it came to having a social life.

"We'll have to remedy that," Sonja said. "Let's make it a point to have dinner again soon." The two had gone out to dinner shortly after Anna moved to Seagull Cove, and Anna had enjoyed getting to know Sonja.

"It's funny you should suggest that, because I was recently talking with Ruthie Valentino, and we were saying that it would be nice for all three of us to get together, along with Rosie DeLuca, who owns the *Inn at Seagull Cove*. Maybe the four of us could have dinner next month."

"That would be wonderful," Sonja said. "It will be something to look forward to."

"Hopefully by then there will be no more murder mysteries to solve," Anna added.

Sonja gave Anna a puzzled look. "Don't tell me you're involved in solving another murder? Wait. Are you talking about Luke Carter?"

Oops.

Anna hadn't meant to let that slip, but there was no harm done. She trusted Sonja. Sonja wasn't the type to gossip.

"Promise me you won't tell anyone. Ellen and I already got ourselves into trouble with Charlie Doyle, and plus, if Joe Wiggins hears that I'm investigating again, he'll never let me hear the end of it."

"I won't tell anyone." Sonja gave her a playful smile. "That is, if you tell me who your suspects are. All I do is work and sleep. I could use some interesting news."

Anna chuckled. She filled Sonja in on who their suspects had been and where things stood now with each of them. "Basically, we're now focusing all of our attention on Philip Pearson."

Sonja appeared to be thinking. "What does Philip look like?"

"I'd say he's about thirty-five, brown messy hair, average height," Anna said.

Sonja was silent. "That sounds like the guy who was in here with Luke a few days before Luke's death." Sonja paused. "Yes, it *was* Friday afternoon. I remember, because it's the last time I saw Luke. His office was right across the street, so he was a regular here, and I remember thinking after he died that that was the last time I saw him. Luke often would come in for a coffee when he wanted to take an afternoon break or sometimes to meet with a client. The two of them were sitting in the back of my coffee shop and were deep in conversation. I felt badly, because I didn't even say hello to Luke. I didn't want to interrupt their conversation but now I wish I had. It turned out to be the last time I saw him."

"What was the tone of their encounter?" Anna asked.

"They appeared to be angry. I didn't hear why, but they were sitting across from one another, and they were clearly discussing something of significance. They both seemed unhappy about whatever it was they were discussing."

"Did Philip seem angry at Luke, or was Luke angry with Philip?"

"I'd have to say that Philip appeared to be the angry one. Luke seemed frustrated. But it was hard to tell from a distance. All I can say for certain was that it wasn't a social visit. It had more of a formal, business-type feel. They were here for about twenty minutes before they left together. If I had realized that Luke would be murdered shortly after, I obviously would have paid closer attention. I figured Philip was a client. I'm afraid I haven't been much help. I can't even tell you if it was Philip for sure."

"You've been more helpful than you realize. It sounds like

Ellen and I need to talk to Philip again. He conveniently left out his conversation with Luke three days before Luke was killed."

"Be careful," Sonja said. "He sounds like a dangerous dude."

"We always are."

After her visit with Sonja, Anna got into work a little bit early, so she called Ellen and filled her in on what she just learned.

"Are you kidding me?" Ellen asked. "Philip had coffee with Luke three days before Luke died and he neglected to mention that to us?"

"Sonja couldn't be one-hundred percent sure that it was Philip, but based on my description of Philip, there's a pretty good chance it was."

"We need to find out for sure if it was Philip. But how can we do that?"

Anna thought for a moment. "I'm not sure. I have to open the store in fifteen minutes, but can you meet later so we can come up with a plan?"

"I can come by the shop in the early afternoon."

"Perfect. I should be able to break away. I'll see you later."

As the morning and early afternoon wore on, the temperature climbed into the high eighties, which kept foot traffic high. There was nothing like a hot day to put people in the mood for ice cream.

When Ellen came by right after lunch, Anna left Velma in charge of the rest of the staff and went for a walk with Ellen so they could discuss their next move.

CHAPTER 24

Anna and Ellen strolled in the direction of the beaches. The fresh, salty air was invigorating.

"I'm glad we decided to go for a walk," Anna said. "It's such a beautiful day."

"Me, too. My younger children are in camp all month, so I have more free time than usual during the day. With Luke's death, it's been hard to enjoy the simple pleasures in life."

"I don't think your brother would want you to be cooped up inside all summer."

"True. But that's easier said than done," Ellen said.

Anna's heart grew heavy. "Trust me, I understand."

"Besides, it's hard to have any peace while my brother's killer is still out there. I want to make sure the right person ends up behind bars. Then, I'll work on healing and trying to find some joy this summer."

"I want that for you, too," Anna said. "Speaking of which, we need to decide what to do next."

"I wish we could ask Philip directly what he was doing with my brother."

"Me, too. But if we did that, he'd know that we're on to him. That might not be the smartest move, especially if he turns out to be the killer. We'd not only be putting ourselves in danger, but he'd probably go to Charlie again, which would shut down our investigation."

"But if he's *not* the killer, and he and Luke were talking about something else, it would be useful for us to know why they were meeting."

"That's a good point. It's a tough call," Ellen said. "I called Nicole earlier. She didn't know anything about their meeting."

"Maybe we can trick him into revealing the conversation to us," Anna said.

As the women passed the cove, which was dotted with colorful beach blankets and umbrellas, they noticed Joe Wiggins walking in their direction up ahead.

Anna smiled and waved as he approached. "Joe must be out for his afternoon walk. He is as predictable as the sunrise. He's probably headed to *Bella's Dream* for his daily scoop of chocolate chip ice cream."

"Hello, ladies," Joe said, tapping the inside rim of his Red Sox cap. "It's a beautiful day for a stroll along the beach." He held Anna's gaze for a moment.

Just seeing him made her feel guilty that they were investigating again, after she told him they weren't. Of course, both times that she denied any involvement, they were not actually investigating. But she still felt uneasy.

"Just lovely," Ellen said.

"It's nice to see the two of you becoming fast friends," Joe said.

"Having the opportunity to get to know Anna has been

one of the few positive things that has happened since my brother's death," Ellen said.

"Our Anna is a welcomed addition to the Seagull Cove community, even if she *does* have a knack for getting into trouble. I hope she's not rubbing off on you," Joe said with a playful smile, but the serious look in his eyes told Anna that he wasn't completely teasing her.

"Oh, I'm not looking for trouble. I'm just a mom of three who has all she can do to keep up with her kids."

"Uh-huh," Joe said with a twinkle in his blue eyes as he continued on his way.

The two women had to laugh when Joe was out of earshot.

"Oh, he is totally on to us," Ellen said.

"If there's one thing that I know about Joe Wiggins, it's that you can't get much past him."

The women continued walking past the cove and towards Mile Long Beach.

"Getting back to Philip," Anna said, "I think I have an idea. What if we could set some sort of trap that would tell us if he's the killer?"

"Hmm, that's an interesting idea, but what kind of trap?"

Anna searched her mind for an idea. "Well, we know that he is being investigated for arson. What if we could find a way to trick him into thinking that we have proof that he is guilty?"

The women turned around and started walking back in the direction of *Bella's Dream*. They each remained silent for a few minutes. When they reached the cove, they stopped and sat on the cement wall, which separated the beach from the promenade.

"How on earth would we do that?" Ellen finally asked. "It's

a lost cause. If we talk to Philip, we'll put ourselves in danger, or at the very least, get ourselves into trouble with Charlie. If we don't, the police might waste their time on Chris while the real killer walks free."

"That's exactly why our only option is to set a trap for Philip. But what kind?" Anna asked, thinking aloud. Then a moment later, she exclaimed, "I've got it!"

Ellen looked wide-eyed at Anna.

"What if we got word to Philip that we have evidence that proves who set fire to his house? We could make up a story, saying that this proof is in Luke's office. Philip would definitely want to get his hands on the fictitious evidence that would implicate him, and we could be waiting for him when he arrives. We'll catch him in the act."

"How would we get that information to Philip?" Ellen asked.

"Nicole could call him and say that she came across a message in Luke's files saying he had evidence in his office that could lead to the arsonist. Then tell him she's going to look for the file at Luke's office the next morning to give him time to try to intercept it."

"But why would Nicole contact Philip if she believed that he was guilty? He'd never believe that," Ellen said.

"Philip doesn't know that *we* know that his alibi fell through. He might believe that Nicole would confide in him if she believed he couldn't possibly be the killer."

"Hmm, that could work. The only problem I can see is that we'd have to spend the night in the office to see if Philip showed up. That could be dangerous," Ellen pointed out. "I'd have a hard time convincing Caleb to let me do *that*."

"Good point." Anna reflected for another moment. "What

if we didn't have to do a stakeout? We could set up a camera and watch from a distance. That would be even better, because if Philip showed up and searched Luke's office, we would have it recorded. Then we could send the video to Charlie. It wouldn't prove that Philip killed Luke, but at least it would give the police another reason to investigate Philip further instead of staying focused on Chris."

"I like it. I'll call Nicole and see if she's willing to do it," Ellen said, taking her phone from her purse and placing the call.

It didn't take much convincing.

"Nicole said she'd do anything to catch Luke's killer," Ellen said, after disconnecting the call with Nicole. "I told her to come by your ice cream shop in the morning before work so she could call from there. That way we can give her some moral support. Can you meet us at your shop at 8:15? That will give me time to drop the kids off at camp, and it will give Nicole enough time to make it to work by 9:00."

"Absolutely," Anna said. "I'll see you then."

When Anna returned to *Bella's Dream*, Joe was sitting at the counter savoring his ice cream. She didn't want him to ask about her conversation with Ellen, because she knew she wouldn't be able to lie to him. So, she pretended she had some administrative work to do and went into her office.

Once she got her evening shift employees settled in, Anna took the evening off.

CHAPTER 25

Anna took the long way home from work, turning right onto Main Street and detouring through several residential neighborhoods. As she strolled through the quintessential New England neighborhoods, with their quaint wooden cottages and white picket fences, it wasn't to Luke's case that her mind wandered. Instead, she thought of her conversation with Grayson, and of the information she had uncovered about Bella's credit card debt. Or rather, *lack* of credit card debt.

Anna also wondered why Bella had begun classes to become a nail technician without breathing a word about it to Anna. It was just one more missing piece of the puzzle. Anna and Bella spent so much time together, both at work and outside of work, that they talked about everything. There's no way Bella wouldn't have mentioned that to Anna unless she was deliberately trying to hide it.

Then there was the swim training. Anna might be inclined to believe that Bella's swim training was simply something that never came up if she hadn't directly lied to Grayson about canceling her gym membership.

The more Anna thought about it, the more it became clear that for Anna not to have known about the nail technician classes, Bella would have had to have gone to great effort to hide the fact that she was taking them. According to Grayson, her weekly classes took place on Thursday evenings. Anna and Bella often had dinner on Fridays after work or went to Bella's favorite ice cream shop after their last client of the day. There would have been plenty of opportunities for Bella to talk about it, and there was no logical reason for her to hide it.

The more Anna thought about it, the more she realized that this seemingly small thing was just as strange, if not more so, than the missing retirement money and the swim lessons.

By the time Anna got home, she was more convinced than ever that she needed to move forward full force to find out the answers to her questions.

Anna took her laptop into the living room and settled in on her couch. She did an Internet search for "beauty schools," and a website popped up outlining the steps necessary to become a licensed nail technician. She imagined herself as Bella, more than four years ago. If Bella needed to make it appear as if she were dead, she would need to start a new life under a different name. She wouldn't be able to rely on her license as a counselor, because she would need to leave behind her old identity.

Anna shivered at the thought of her sister going through so much while Anna knew nothing about it. But she pushed through her uneasiness and continued reading.

Becoming a nail technician would be something Bella could

get certified in relatively quickly, at least compared to obtaining another counseling degree and licensing. Perhaps that's why Bella chose this path. She enjoyed working with people, and, if nothing else, a nail technician license would provide her with a skill with which to begin her new life. Anna tried to imagine Bella working in a salon. Bella was an extrovert, so it was easy to picture her taking care of others in this way and connecting with her clients. She also loved to try new things.

According to Anna's research, it appeared that, while some of the details varied from state to state, there were generally three steps to obtaining a license: apply to and complete a program, pass the licensing exam, and complete supervised hours. Even if Bella hadn't completed the program before her boating accident, taking at least part of the course would put her a little ahead of the game if she were relocating. All in all, it would likely take about a year to complete. And Bella certainly had enough money from her retirement and savings accounts to pay for the course and cover her expenses while she got on her feet. Especially if she relocated to a more remote location where the cost of living was low. With all the publicity that her boating accident received, Anna imagined that Bella would have chosen a more out-of-the-way location. Perhaps central or northern Maine or New Hampshire. It would be ironic if Bella had chosen New Hampshire, where her parents had recently retired.

If Joe truly *did* see Bella on the morning of the grand opening, that could very well mean that Bella was within driving distance of Seagull Cove.

Anna shook her head. It was so strange to think of Bella living a life that Anna knew nothing about. They had known everything about each other's lives since the day Bella was born. At least Anna thought they had.

That reminded Anna to text Grayson to get one last piece of information from him.

Hey, Grayson. It was great seeing you Sunday! Would you happen to remember the name or location of the nail technician school where my sister was taking classes? Also, do you happen to remember when she started the class?

Grayson's reply came within a few seconds. *Sorry, Anna. She never mentioned the name of the school. I just remember that her class was on a Thursday night. She hadn't been taking the classes long. She only started in July.*

Thanks, Grayson.

If she only started the course three months before her accident, Bella wouldn't have nearly had time to complete it. Maybe she was just testing it out to see if she liked it. Of course, there was also the possibility that Anna was wasting her time. It all could have been an innocent misunderstanding if Bella was only taking the course as a hobby. But then, why wouldn't Bella have told Anna about it? If it were only a hobby, she would have dragged Anna along, whether Anna had any interest or not. That's what usually happened when Bella discovered a new interest.

Anna had stuffed the boxes filled with Bella's financial paperwork into the closet in her guest bedroom, rather than taking them back upstairs, in case she wanted to consult them again. She pulled out the box that contained Bella's credit card statements and perused them again, going back a year before Bella's death. There weren't any charges to anything that resembled a beauty school on any of the statements. Next, Anna went through her bank statements, just in case Bella had paid for the course using her debit card. Again, nothing. She must have paid in cash. That was another sign that Bella wanted to take the course in secret. She guessed that Bella had been forced to confide in Grayson, because Thursday night was their date night, so there was probably no way to avoid telling him. But Grayson *did* say that Bella had asked him not to tell anyone.

Before putting away the boxes, Anna decided to try one last thing. She looked up a random nail technician school in Boston and called the number on the website.

"Hello, my name is Anna, and I was looking for some information on your nail technician program."

A friendly voice replied on the other end of the phone. "Sure, what questions can I answer for you?"

"I'm just doing some preliminary research. I don't have any experience in this area, but I may be looking for a career change, and cosmetology has always interested me. The thing is, I might be moving out of state. If I started with your program, would I be able to transfer my credits to another school?"

"What we recommend for people in your situation is to take the course now and hold off on the licensing exam until you relocate. Depending on the state, you might be able to skip the coursework, and with the experience you'd gain with us, you could apply for training hours with a certified technician. You would have to log a certain number of hours, then you could apply for your license in that state."

"Perfect," Anna said. "That's what I was hoping you'd say. Thank you for your time."

Anna's heart rate increased. The secret nail technician course might not have been a big deal on its own. But if you added to that Joe, with his keen observation skills, thinking he saw Bella on the day of Anna's grand opening, Bella lying about closing out her retirement account to pay off credit card debt, the swim training, and now the fact that Bella kept the course a secret, it all seemed to point to the fact that Bella was preparing to start a new life. For the first time since she moved to Seagull Cove, Anna permitted herself to believe that her idea was not just a crazy pipe dream.

The odds of Bella being alive were increasing.

CHAPTER 26

With thoughts of two mysteries still buzzing around in her head, Anna tossed and turned for most of the night. While she was having breakfast on Tuesday morning, Anna determined that she would relay to Charlie the information she had discovered about Bella in hopes that he might at least be able to offer some advice. At best, she hoped he might do some investigating of his own.

After a quick breakfast, Anna walked to *Bella's Dream* to meet Ellen and Nicole as planned. Nicole was glad to not be using her own phone to call Philip, since she didn't want a potential killer to have her phone number. After several minutes of coaching from Anna and Ellen, Nicole took a deep breath and placed the call.

"Hi, Philip, this is Nicole Teagan. I worked for Luke Carter." There was a brief pause before she continued. "Yes, that's me. Listen, this is just a courtesy call. I wanted to let you know that I was going through some of Luke's files, and I saw a note that was written in Luke's handwriting. It indicated that he had some sort of evidence, which he left in the file cabinet in the office, proving who started the fire at your house. I just discovered it a short time ago and haven't yet had a chance to go by Luke's office to check it out, but I thought you'd want to know."

There was a pause while Nicole listened. "Of course I don't believe that *you* did it. Otherwise, I wouldn't be telling you what I found. I know that you have an alibi. I just thought you'd want to know that your nightmare might soon be over. I'm going to go by Luke's office first thing tomorrow morning to start clearing it out, and to see if I can find the evidence he was talking about. But I wanted to tell you the good news right away. With any luck, by tomorrow we'll know who did this to you."

Anna and Ellen waited with bated breath for Nicole to hang up.

"I think he bought my story," Nicole said after she finally disconnected the call. "But it wasn't the reaction I expected."

"Did he sound nervous?" Anna asked.

"Not exactly. He said that he doubted that Luke had any evidence that could clear him, or Luke would have taken it to the police."

"Of course he'd say that," Anna said. "If he plans to steal the evidence tonight, then by tomorrow morning, the evidence will have disappeared."

"I suppose you could be right," Nicole said.

"We'll know soon enough. If Philip is guilty of starting the fire, then he'll be at Luke's office tonight looking for that evidence," Anna said.

"True enough."

"Charlie mentioned that Luke's security camera wasn't working the morning of Luke's murder. We need to set up a camera ASAP so we can see if Philip tries to find this fictitious evidence," Anna said.

Ellen shook her head. "There's no need to do that. I had Luke's security camera repaired, and I have the software on my laptop. I figured you never know if the killer will return to the scene of the crime."

"Perfect," Anna said. "It sounds like all that's left to do is wait to see if Philip shows up."

"Are you two going to stay up all night to watch what happens, or just look at the footage in the morning?" Nicole asked.

"Personally, I'd love to wait up and watch from my shop, but Joe might see my lights on and come downstairs. Let's regroup in the morning and go over the footage," Anna said.

"I guess you're right. Besides, I don't think I could convince my husband to let me spend the night in your shop, anyway."

"It's settled then," Anna said.

"Call me in the morning, as soon as you have any news," Nicole said. "I can't wait to hear what happens."

With their plans firmly in place, the women each went their separate ways.

Since it was still early, Anna returned home to water her garden and pull a few weeds before beginning her workday. After puttering around in her yard for a little while, she washed up and enjoyed a second cup of coffee on the porch. The brightly-colored vegetation had a way of cheering Anna up, as she often found her thoughts drifting to murder and missing-person investigations these days.

As she walked to work a little later, Anna wondered

whether she had found enough circumstantial evidence to convince Charlie that Bella could still be alive.

She just *had* to know. As soon as she arrived at her shop, she sat in the dining room and called Charlie.

"Charlie, it's Anna McBride. I was hoping we could talk for a few minutes, today if possible."

"Hi, Anna. I suppose I could squeak out a few minutes this afternoon, but if this is about the murder investigation, I don't have any news, so it would be a waste of both of our time."

"It has nothing to do with that," Anna assured him.

"In that case, I'll stop by *Bella's Dream* as soon as I can. It probably won't be until the afternoon."

"I'll be here all day," Anna said.

Velma, Olivia, Jack, and Alex arrived right on time for their shifts, and the store was busy almost from the time they opened. When Charlie walked in the door, Anna couldn't believe it was already the afternoon.

"Can I get you a scoop on the house?" Anna asked.

"That's an offer I can't turn down," Charlie said with a smile.

Anna put a scoop of chocolate, Charlie's favorite, into a cup. Then Charlie spotted a group of local teenagers having an ice cream.

"Do you mind if I join them for a few minutes before we talk?" Charlie asked. "They are friends of my oldest son, and I like to spend a little time with them when I can. I want them to feel they can come to me if they ever need to."

"Take your time," Anna said.

Anna watched Charlie with the teenagers.

"I think I'm going to be a detective when I grow up," one of them said with a playful smirk. "You get to eat ice cream every day."

Charlie was obviously doing a great job putting off an approachable vibe if they felt comfortable teasing him like that. Anna smiled and helped her employees behind the counter while she waited for Charlie to finish. Then they went out back into Anna's office.

"Thanks for waiting," Charlie said. "What is it I can help you with?"

Anna took a deep breath. "It's about my sister, Bella."

Charlie looked surprised. "What about Bella?"

Anna recounted everything that had happened since her grand opening - Joe spotting someone who looked like Anna, the financial records, the swim training, and the nail technician classes.

Charlie's face grew solemn.

"Anna, I know..."

Anna cut him off. "Please don't tell me that it's normal for me to miss my sister and that this must be all in my imagination."

"I would never do that."

"We were so close, Charlie. We were Irish twins, and we shared a counseling practice together. We knew *everything* about each other. Why would my sister lie about her finances and hide her swim training and her nail technician course from me if she didn't have a reason? It doesn't make any sense. And don't forget, her body was never found."

Charlie looked thoughtfully at Anna but didn't say a word.

"Even Joe said that if it were his sister, he would need to find the answers to these questions," she added, shamelessly hoping Joe's name would give her theory some credibility.

"Anna, I wish I could help you, even if it was just to put your mind at ease and address your doubts about your sister's death. But I am the only detective in this town, and I currently have a murder to solve. All of your evidence is circumstantial. None of it is something that I can justify the time and resources it would take to investigate. I'm sorry."

Anna's heart sank. "I guess I can understand that. But what am I going to do? I can't live with these doubts."

"Is Joe willing to help you?" Charlie asked.

"He came with me to look at the site of the accident, and he has been a wonderful sounding board. But I don't think he'd come out of retirement to investigate full-time."

"Then your best bet might be to hire another P.I. If he or she could uncover some solid evidence, maybe we could talk again. But I would need something *very* solid to take to my lieutenant."

"I understand." Anna had mixed feelings about Charlie's response. She was happy that he didn't try to shut her down completely and treat her like a foolish, overly hopeful, sister. But at the same time, she really had hoped that he might investigate. With Charlie's experience and resources, he would be able to get to the bottom of things a lot faster than Anna could. And a private investigator would likely be costly.

"I mean it about hiring a professional," Charlie said. "I know you need answers, but even if Bella were somehow alive, that would mean she staged her death, and that would require an extremely compelling reason. Anna, either your sister is alive and is entangled in a very dangerous situation, or she isn't and you're setting yourself up for a major disappointment."

Charlie didn't say anything that Anna didn't already know,

but she appreciated that he at least took her dilemma seriously.

The only solution Anna could see was to investigate herself. She couldn't afford a private investigator. Besides, nobody knew Bella like Anna did. If anyone could figure out what happened, it was Anna. She doubted that Joe would take the lead on this case, but she was counting on her assumption that he wouldn't leave her totally high and dry.

"I understand, Charlie. I am going into this with my eyes wide open. I will take everything you said into consideration." Anna refused to make any false promises to Charlie.

After Charlie left, the rest of the day flew by. She ended the night by feeding Casper. The poor little cat still looked melancholy. Anna guessed that he missed his friend, Luke. "We are doing everything we can to get justice for Luke," Anna said as she scratched the top of his orange head. Hopefully, we will come closer to having some answers by the morning."

It took her a long time to fall asleep that night. It was hard not to wonder if Philip was going to break into Luke's office that night. However, shortly after midnight, she managed to drift off to sleep.

At 6:00 the following morning Anna was awakened by a phone call. It was Ellen.

She jumped out of bed and took the call in her living room.

"Hi Ellen, any news?"

"Oh, I've got some news, alright. Someone broke into Luke's office, but it wasn't Philip."

CHAPTER 27

"Wait, what?!" Anna replied. "If not Philip, then who broke into Luke's office?"

"You have to see this in person. Can you meet me at *Bella's Dream* in ten minutes? I have to run an errand downtown, so I'm already heading in that direction," Ellen said.

"I'm leaving now. Hurry! The suspense is killing me."

Within ten minutes, Ellen was parking in front of Anna's shop. With her laptop tucked under her arm, she raced toward the door, where Anna was waiting for her. Ellen set up her computer on one of the bistro tables and pulled a chair next to Anna. "Here's the file."

Ellen clicked on the video and it began playing on her screen. The first two minutes didn't show much of anything. The camera was focused on Luke's desk, and most of the office was in view.

"Nothing's happening. Are you sure you didn't erase it by accident?" Anna asked.

"I'm positive. Just give it another minute."

After what seemed like an eternity, but in reality was only

about twenty seconds, the doorknob on the back door slowly turned, and the door creaked open.

The person entering put something into their pocket.

"I think that was a credit card that she used to open the door. Luke's locks were horrible, but he never felt the need to invest in better ones, because he didn't keep anything of value in his office."

"She?" Anna asked.

"Yes. Watch."

The woman was tall and thin, wearing a black sweatshirt and black yoga pants. She reminded Anna of someone she had seen before, but she couldn't figure out who.

The woman walked over to the front of Luke's desk and shuffled through some papers. Then she walked around to the other side and her face finally came into view.

It was Loni Devereaux.

"Of course!" Anna cried. "It makes perfect sense."

"It's not over yet," Ellen said. "Listen."

Loni examined some more papers on Luke's desk, snapping some pictures of various documents with her cell phone.

"Where is it, Luke?" Loni muttered. "Even in death you're making my life difficult." She opened the file cabinet and poured through the folders." Then she looked around frantically. "Where is your computer? Shoot. It had better not be on your computer, Luke."

After searching every square inch of the office, Loni finally left through the fire escape, the same way she had come in.

Anna looked at Ellen, speechless.

"It looks like your plan worked," Ellen said. "Now we know who started the fire at Philip's house. I'm guessing she did it to put my brother out of business. Do you think she killed Luke, too?"

"I'd say there's a pretty good chance."

"We have to get this video file to the police," Ellen said.

Anna stared at the screen for a moment, and a terrifying thought occurred to her. "If Loni is searching for Luke's computer to find this fictitious evidence, there's a good chance she'll start with Nicole. We need to call her right away."

"That's a good point," Ellen said, shutting her laptop. "But let's not call. Let's go to Nicole's house and check on her in person."

Anna's heart raced. "The sooner, the better. Setting a trap was my idea. I wouldn't be able to live with myself if our sleuthing put her in danger."

"It's only 7:00. Nicole is probably just waking up for work," Ellen said.

The two women hopped into Ellen's car and raced across town. As they were driving, the hair on Anna's arms stood up. She turned around and looked out the rear window of Ellen's car. There was a black Honda Civic a short distance behind them.

"I feel like that car is following us."

Ellen turned off Main Street into a residential neighborhood, and sure enough, the black car also turned. A few minutes later, Ellen turned one last time. "This is Nicole's house."

It was a grey cottage, about a mile from Main Street. There was a car parked in Nicole's driveway, as well as two others on the street in front of her house.

"Do you recognize those cars?" Anna asked.

"The one in the driveway belongs to Nicole. I don't recognize the others," Ellen said, parking behind the two cars on the street. "What should we do?"

"I'm going to take a walk around Nicole's house to make sure everything's okay."

"I'm coming with you," Ellen said. "I got you into this mess by asking you to help find my brother's killer. We're in this together."

After they exited Ellen's car, Anna glanced at the street behind them. The black Honda was now parked twenty yards behind them on the opposite side of the street.

"There's that car again," Anna said. "That person *has* to be following us."

"Should we check it out before we go to Nicole's?"

Anna shook her head. "Let's make sure Nicole is okay first. Then we'll see what's up with that car. I doubt it's Loni. It doesn't look like a car she would drive."

"Good thinking. Judging from the jewelry she was wearing when we went to her office, Loni probably drives a more expensive luxury car."

The two women snuck around to the back of Nicole's house.

"Shouldn't we ring the doorbell? We might scare Nicole if she sees us creeping around her yard," Ellen said.

"If one of those cars belongs to Loni, we don't want to tip her off that we're here. If something looks amiss, we'll call the police." Anna could only imagine the flack she would take if they had to call the police because they put Nicole in danger with their sleuthing.

Ellen pointed to a window in the back of the house. "I think that window leads to her bedroom," Ellen said.

"The blinds are closed. We won't be able to see anything."

"The living room is on the other side of the house. Let's check to see if we can see anything through that window."

They crept around to the other side of the house and approached the living room window. As Anna was about to look inside, she felt a firm hand grasp her shoulder. The hand was too large to belong to Ellen.

Ellen gasped loudly behind her.

Anna slowly turned around. The hand belonged to Philip. And his other hand was grasping Ellen's shoulder.

Anna turned abruptly to try to free herself from his grip, but he grabbed her arm instead of letting go and pulled Anna and Ellen to the side of a small, detached garage. He finally released them. "What are you two doing here?" he whispered.

"Checking on Nicole. More importantly, what are *you* doing here, Philip?" Ellen asked.

Philip studied the two women for a moment until a look of recognition dawned on his face. "Wait, was Nicole setting me up when she told me that story about Luke having evidence proving who set the fire at my house?" He shook his head. "I should have known."

"I'm still confused," Ellen said. "It was Loni who broke into Luke's office this morning. I still don't understand what *you* are doing here."

"I'm doing the same thing as you - trying to find out who set fire to my house. I'll explain later," Philip said. "Right now, we need to call the police. Just before you got here, Loni entered Nicole's house."

Anna sprinted toward Nicole's cottage, determined not to let anything happen to the innocent young woman, since this whole idea of a stakeout had been hers.

As she was running, Anna heard Ellen's voice call out behind her. "You can't go in there alone." When Anna arrived at the back porch, she turned around. Ellen and Philip weren't far behind.

Anna opened the French doors, which were unlocked, and found Loni creeping around the house, presumably looking for Luke's computer. Loni turned around when she heard Anna enter, then she bolted in the direction of the front door.

Loni grasped the doorknob and swung the door wide open.

Anna was right behind her. She had caught up to Loni and threw up her hands to prevent the wooden door from hitting her in the head.

Just as Loni was about to take off down the front stairs, Anna grabbed her from behind and yanked her away from the front staircase.

Loni struggled to break free, and it was all Anna could do to hold on to her. Just as she was about to lose her grip, Philip grabbed Loni and pulled her back into Nicole's house. The unlikely trio surrounded Loni and closed in on her, until Anna grabbed her around the waist.

Philip then wrestled Loni into a headlock and dragged her into the middle of the living room, away from the front and back doors. "You can let go of her, Anna. I have her good."

Just as they were apprehending Loni, a confused Nicole emerged from her bedroom, wearing a silk lavender bathrobe. Her sleepy eyes flew wide open when she saw her four unexpected visitors in her living room.

"What on earth are you all doing here?!" she asked, aghast.

"We'll explain all that in a few minutes," Anna said. "For now, we have to call the police."

Nicole grabbed her landline phone, which was right next to her on the kitchen counter, but was interrupted by yet a fourth unexpected guest.

"There's no need. I already called the police."

It was Joe Wiggins.

"You are a lot of work, Anna McBride."

CHAPTER 28

Anna stared at Joe Wiggins while she tried to process the situation.

"It was *you* who was following us in the black Honda Civic." Anna had never seen Joe's car before, which was why she didn't recognize it. Her thoughts flashed back to when Nina accused Anna of breaking her promise and telling the police about Scout. "And it was *you* who put the police on to Scout."

"Guilty as charged," Joe said. "I was sitting on my porch on Monday evening when you left your shop and headed to the beach. You looked like a woman on a mission, and my gut told me you were up to something, so I followed you. I saw you meet Nina and her friend at the cove, so I had Charlie send out a deputy to keep an eye on them. And then tonight I saw you come into *Bella's Dream* five hours before the shop opens. I knew something was up when Ellen arrived shortly after you with her laptop under her arm."

"So, you followed us here."

"Yup. Someone's got to keep an eye on Seagull Cove's

amateur sleuth." At least Joe didn't look upset. In fact, Anna was relieved that everything was out in the open. She hated to do things behind Joe's back.

Anna gave Joe a hug, causing him to blush. He patted her on the back. "Right back at you, kiddo."

Then Joe stood by Philip and Loni to ensure that Loni didn't try anything funny.

Within a couple of minutes, there was a pounding on Nicole's front door.

"Nicole, it's the police. Are you okay in there?"

Nicole opened the door, still appearing to be shell-shocked from her unusual morning, and in came Detective Charlie Doyle, along with another police officer.

"Could someone explain to me what's going on?" Charlie asked.

"I don't know the whole story, but I *do* know that this woman broke into my house," Nicole said, pointing to Loni, "and these other folks apprehended her. I suspect she was looking for the evidence, which she believed Luke had, that proved she is the one who set fire to Philip's house."

"Ellen has proof that Loni broke into Luke's office early this morning. And if you ask me, she killed Luke because she knew he could prove that she started the fire," Anna added.

"I saw Loni break into this house with my own eyes," Philip said.

"I certainly didn't invite her in," Nicole said.

"We'll sort all this out at the police station. You're coming with me," he said to Loni. "And I'll need the rest of you to meet me there, as well." Charlie escorted Loni out the door in handcuffs.

After they left, Nicole held up her hand. "Hold on, everyone. Before we go to the police station, could you explain how you ended up in my house this morning? I heard how Joe ended up here, but what about the rest of you?"

"I'd like to know the whole story myself," Joe said.

Anna and Ellen looked at one another.

"Fair enough," Anna said.

Nicole brewed a large pot of coffee, and Ellen poured a mug for everyone while Nicole changed out of her night clothes.

When she returned and joined the others in the living room, Anna began explaining. "Philip, I'm sorry to say that as of yesterday, you were our prime suspect in Luke's murder."

"We thought you were guilty of arson and that Luke had evidence to prove it. That's why we thought you killed him," Ellen said.

Philip ran his hand through his messy brown hair. "So, I was right. When you told me that there was evidence in Luke's office proving who set my house on fire, you thought I'd go searching for it, because you believed I was guilty."

"Exactly," Anna said. "We were trying to set you up."

"Unfortunately," Philip said, "I called Loni shortly after Nicole called me and told her that this nightmare might finally be behind me, because apparently there was evidence in Luke's office that could clear me of arson. It didn't occur to me until later that Loni might actually be the guilty party."

"Ellen had the camera in Luke's office repaired, and you can imagine our surprise when Loni was the one who broke in, frantically searching for the fictitious evidence," Ellen said.

"Except that I'm not convinced that the evidence was fictitious," Anna said.

Ellen furrowed her brow. "What do you mean?"

"Nicole really *did* find a note that said that Luke had evidence of who started the fire. We just don't know where that evidence is," Anna said.

"That's what led me to suspect Loni. After I called her and told her what Nicole told me, I remembered a conversation that Luke and I had."

"The one that took place at *Cove Coffee* the Friday before Luke died?" Anna asked

Philip looked surprised. "I didn't think anyone knew about that."

"Sonja, the owner of the coffee shop, is a friend of mine. She told me that the two of you met and appeared to be having a heated discussion."

"We were," Philip said. "Luke told me that day that he suspected it was Loni who set the fire. He said he had some type of audio file as evidence. At that point, I had left Luke, and Loni was my new agent. I thought his theory sounded ridiculous and that it was a pathetic ploy to get me back as a client. I walked out before he could finish telling me his farfetched theory. At least I believed it was farfetched at the time. After Nicole called me, I got to thinking. Loni complained a lot about young, up-and-coming agents cutting into her business, and I considered that maybe Luke was right. So, I did a stakeout of my own. I waited in my car across the street from Luke's office, and what I'd hoped *wouldn't* happen, happened. Loni appeared. When she left Luke's office, I followed her here. I didn't understand why she came here, and I didn't even know it was Nicole's house until the two of you arrived," he said to Anna and Ellen. "But I knew she was up to no good."

"She came here when she couldn't find the evidence in Luke's office, hoping it might be on his computer," Ellen said.

"It's all my fault. I told Loni that it was Nicole who told me about the evidence. She knew Nicole was Luke's administrative assistant and was closing out Luke's accounts. She probably assumed that Nicole had Luke's computer," Philip said.

"It's not your fault, Philip. It's *my* fault for proposing we set the trap. As soon as we saw the footage of the break-in, we came right here," Anna said.

"Now do you understand why I'm always so worried about you when you decide to get involved in police work?" Joe asked Anna. "Nicole could have gotten hurt. You all could have."

But Nicole came to Anna's defense. "I'm glad they didn't give up. It's as much my fault as anyone else's. I was the one who called Philip, so I was involved, too. I can't thank you all enough for being here. We know that Loni is guilty of arson. Hopefully, it won't be long until the police can prove that Loni is guilty of murder, too."

Philip shook his head. "I can't believe that Loni set my house on fire just to make Luke look bad and put him out of business."

Joe shrugged his shoulders. "It's all about the do-re-mi."

"I hope she goes to prison for a long time," Ellen said.

"I just have one last bone to pick with you, Anna McBride," Joe said, wagging his index finger at Anna. "You told me you and Ellen weren't investigating anymore."

"Well, we *weren't* when you asked me. We really did stop when Charlie asked us to - until Nina pulled us in again, that is." Anna explained how Chris had an alibi that he wouldn't tell the police about, because it involved illegal activity.

"I guess we should get over to the police station. Charlie is probably waiting for us. I'll get my laptop so I can email Charlie the video file of Loni breaking into Luke's office before we leave," Ellen said, disappearing out the front door. A couple of minutes later, she returned with her computer and got to work.

As Anna watched Ellen tap away on her laptop, an idea suddenly occurred to her. "Wait a minute! I just had a thought. Wouldn't it be ironic if Loni was right? What if the evidence Luke had *is* on his computer?"

They stared at one another for a few seconds. Then Nicole disappeared and returned with a computer in hand. "There's only one way to find out. This is Luke's laptop. Let me see what I can find."

Nicole tapped on the keyboard for a few minutes. After a few dead ends, she was about to give up. "Let me try one more search." She tapped furiously on the keyboard. "This might be it. There's something with Loni's name in his audio folder. I've never gone in there, because I didn't know it contained any files."

When Nicole pressed play, Luke's voice bellowed through the speakers of her computer.

First, he stated the date, which was five days before he was killed. Then he added that Loni was coming up the stairs and that he was going to confront her about starting the fire.

A conversation followed in which Luke got Loni to confess that she set the fire at Philip's. Furthermore, she threatened Luke's life, saying that if he ever told anyone what she did, she would kill him.

When the recording stopped, everyone sat in stunned silence.

Philip was the first to speak. "Thanks, buddy. You really did come through for me."

"So, *that* was Luke's evidence," Nicole said.

Ellen shook her head in disbelief. "It was on his computer the whole time."

"Let's get this to Charlie," Joe said. "The sooner he has it, the better."

"Then, I'll be paying a visit to the fire marshal to clear my name, thanks to Luke," Philip said.

* * *

ANNA AND ELLEN were the first to finish giving their statements. Joe was talking to the lieutenant when they left. Philip insisted on staying until Charlie contacted the fire marshal, and officially got his name cleared.

Ellen drove Anna back to *Bella's Dream*, since they had taken Ellen's car to Nicole's house earlier that morning. It was just after 11:00 when they left the police station, so the ice cream shop was already open. Anna had called Velma on her way to the station to briefly explain that she would be late and that she would fill her in on what happened when she got back to the shop.

Olivia was working the day shift, so Ellen came inside so that she could personally deliver the good news to Olivia that her uncle's killer was behind bars.

As Anna got out of Ellen's car, she glanced up Main Street and chuckled at what she saw. There was Casper prancing down the street, looking as if he didn't have a care in the world.

"What's so funny?" Ellen asked.

Anna pointed to Casper. "That cat is something else. I don't know how, but I wouldn't be surprised if he already knows that the killer has been caught."

When they got inside, Anna and Ellen relayed the entire story to Olivia and Velma, while Sarah and Ethan, the other two staff members working that day, handled the counter.

Velma had to laugh when she heard that Joe showed up at Nicole's that morning. "You're not going to hear the end of that for a long time," she said to Anna.

Ellen left to take a walk along the beach and to decompress after a crazy morning, while Anna hopped behind the counter.

About an hour later Joe Wiggins came into the shop.

"Just getting back from the police station?" Anna asked.

"Yes. I saw Ellen's car out front, so I figured you were all in here still talking about our eventful morning."

Velma smirked from behind the register.

Ellen returned from her walk while they were talking.

"I *thought* that was you," Ellen said to Joe. "I saw you as I was coming up Main Street from the beach."

"I hung around the police station for a little while longer to keep Philip company. His name is officially cleared, so he's a happy camper."

"That's great news," Anna said.

"That's not all. When Loni learned about the evidence we brought to the police station, she confessed to everything."

Ellen looked as if she were about to burst into tears.

"Are you okay?" Anna asked.

"I'm thrilled that my brother's killer was caught, but in a way, today serves as a reminder of the senseless way in which he lost his life. Tell me what you learned after we left, Joe. I want to know."

Joe ushered her to a booth, where they could speak privately, and Anna followed.

"There might be a few gaps in the story that I can fill in for you. On the morning Luke was murdered, Loni had arranged to meet with him. She tried to pay him off in exchange for not going to the police. At the time, he didn't have any evidence that Loni knew of. According to Loni, Luke never told her that he recorded their conversation and could prove that she had committed arson. He probably thought he was protecting himself by not telling her about the recording. But she was still afraid that he would go to the police with what he knew. Of course, Luke refused to accept her bribe. On the morning he died, Luke tried to convince Loni to confess her crime and clear Philip's name. Loni figured that it was only a matter of time until Luke went to the police. It was no secret that Luke and Charlie were friends. Loni had seen them having breakfast one morning, and she figured that it was only a matter of time until he told Charlie what he knew. When Luke wouldn't accept her bribe, she killed him with one of the golf clubs in his office, then she left by the fire escape. This was at 8:30 in the morning."

"That means that Luke had only been dead for fifteen minutes when Olivia found his body,"

Anna said.

Joe nodded.

Ellen's eyes had been closed as she listened to Joe recount her brother's final moments. She opened her eyes. "Thank you for telling me, Joe. I needed to know. After a few difficult years, it's ironic that my brother was killed *after* he got his life back on track. But I'm proud of him. I'm glad my daughter remembers her uncle the way he was in the end. That's the Luke I've always known and loved." A smile crept onto Ellen's face. "Speaking of silver linings, while I was taking a walk, I called Wil to tell him the good news. He was thrilled that the killer was caught, and he also had some wonderful news of his own."

Anna and Joe looked at her expectantly.

"Danielle is pregnant. They had an ultrasound this morning, and they are having a boy."

"That's wonderful!" Anna said.

"That's not all. As soon as they left their appointment, they decided to name their son after Luke," she said with a broad smile.

Anna hugged Ellen. "I'm so happy to hear that."

"I can't thank you enough, Anna," Ellen said. "Without you, Loni would still be free."

"Don't go encouraging her," Joe said. "But I *do* have to give credit where credit is due. Anna does seem to have a knack for solving mysteries."

Anna just hoped that this newfound talent wouldn't let her down as she investigated her sister's disappearance. And hopefully, there wouldn't be any more murders in Seagull Cove to distract her from her most important investigation - finding her sister.

THE END... **of Book 2**

What's Next?

Anna's adventures in Seagull Cove are just beginning! Are you ready to find out what happens next?

Next Book in this Series
Salted Caramel Crime (Book 3)
Available on Amazon.

* * *

Make sure you're on Angela's mailing list so you can learn about new releases, sales and exclusive content. As a thank you gift for joining Angela's Readers' Group, you will receive a free copy of *Vacations and Victims*, the prequel to the *Sapphire Beach Cozy Mystery Series*.

Available in ebook and PDF formats at:
BookHip.com/RHFRLNV

STAY IN TOUCH!

Join Angela's Readers' Group so you can learn about new releases, sales, and exclusive content. As a thank you gift, you will receive a free copy of the ebook *Vacations and Victims*, the prequel to the *Sapphire Beach Cozy Mystery Series*.

To join Angela's Readers' Group, enter your email address at: BookHip.com/RHFRLNV

Website:
AngelaKRyan.com

Email:
Angela@AngelaKRyan.com

Facebook:
Facebook.com/AngelaKRyanAuthor

Instagram:
Instagram.com/authorangelakryan/

Post Office:
Angela K. Ryan, John Paul Publishing,
Post Office Box 283, Tewksbury, MA 01876

ABOUT THE AUTHOR

Angela K. Ryan is the author of the *Seaside Ice Cream Shop Mysteries* and the *Sapphire Beach Cozy Mystery Series*. She writes clean, feel-good cozies for readers who love humor, lots of twists and turns, and happy-dance endings.

When she is not writing, Angela enjoys the outdoors, especially kayaking, stand-up paddleboarding, snowshoeing, and skiing. She lives in Massachusetts and loves all four of the New England seasons, but looks forward to regular escapes to the white, sandy beaches of southwest Florida, where her mother resides.

Angela would happily live in either of the fictitious seaside towns in Massachusetts and Florida where her series take place if it weren't for all the bodies that keep turning up!

Angela dreams of one day owning a Cavalier King Charles Spaniel like the sweet pup in her *Sapphire Beach Series*, but she isn't home enough to take care of one. So, for now, she lives vicariously through one of her main characters, Connie.

Made in United States
Orlando, FL
11 July 2024